IMPULSES OF A NECROTIC HEART

DEATH KNELL PRESS

IMPULSES OF A NECROTIC HEART

Cover and interior design by Death Knell Designs
Illustrations by Red Lagoe ©2023
proofread by Donna Hitchcock McCracken

ISBN paperback: 979-8-9873397-2-5
ISBN ebook: 979-8-9873397-3-2

Death Knell Press
www.deathknellpress.com

TABLE OF CONTENTS

INTRODUCTION

Some of the best and worst people in the history of mankind have followed their hearts.

Earlier in the year, when I set out to compile another collection of my short stories, I did the same. It was impulsive. I hadn't planned to release a collection this year, but with such a lapse in time since my last single-author release, I was compelled to do so.

So, I gathered up my stories—some new, some previously published—and I re-visited them. Collectively, I think there's something different about these stories compared to my previous works. There's more *heart* in these characters. There's more loss and tragedy and despair. Most of these stories were written over the past couple of years, and it appears during that time I had found chambers within myself that I don't tend to visit often…I went places I didn't want to go. But once I dipped into that necrotic well of ink, it spilled across everything I wrote.

Many of the stories explore the dark recesses of human nature—those chambers filled with rot that we typically try to avoid. And while there are a few stories that are lighter or even more *fun* in nature, at their core is a dark, pulsing muscle, clinging to hope that it won't fall victim to the spreading infection from neighboring pages.

Pages that include fifteen stories, ranging from sci-fi to psychological, supernatural to body horror, and more. Many were written impulsively, on a whim for some random open call or invite. Yet at the core of every tale, is that palpable, pulsing heart. I hope you feel it too.

From the darkest depths of my necrotic little heart, thank you for reading.

—Red Lagoe

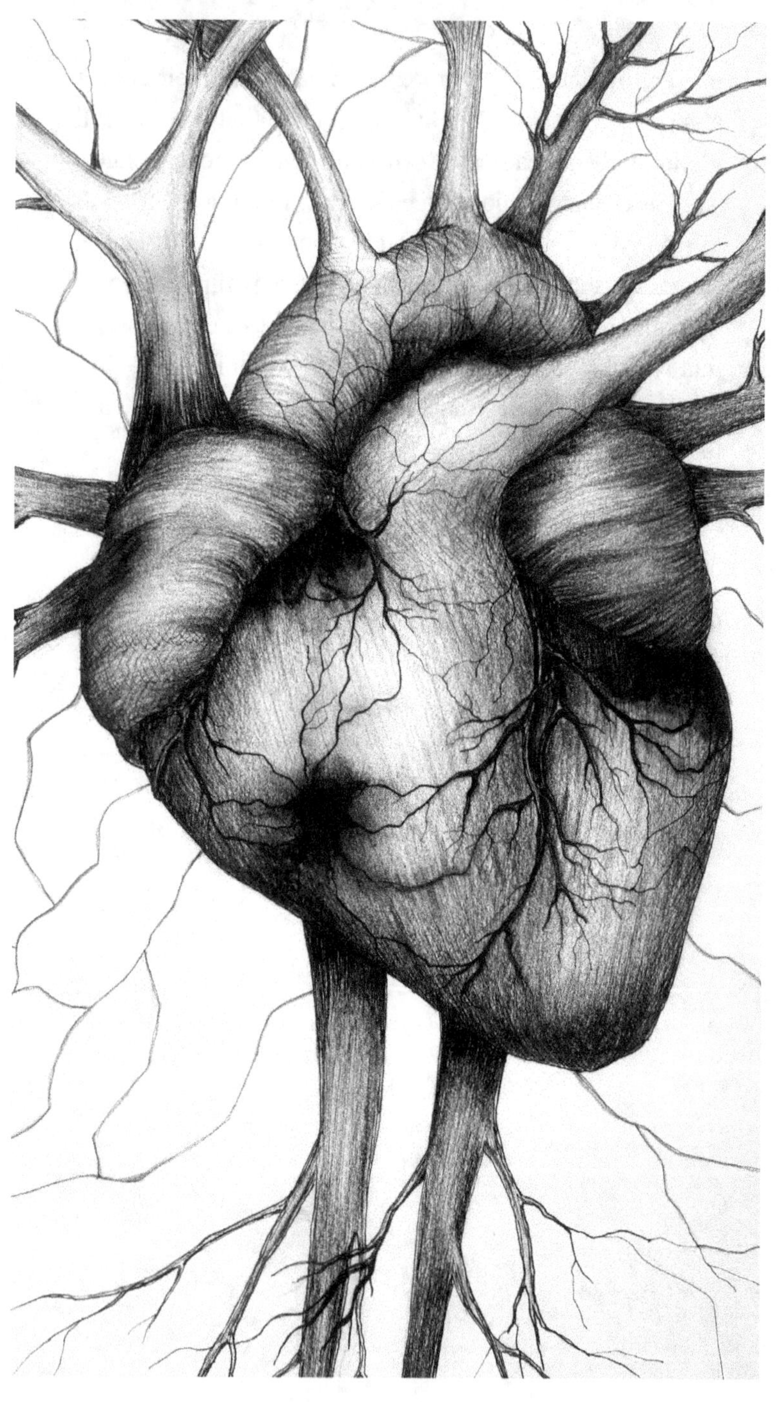

IMPULSES OF A NECROTIC HEART

Dad built an empire with bodies and bullet holes. It was born from hatred and selfishness, and now in his final days, he wished to lay it all at my feet like a carcass. A gutted gift—no more than the shell of a crumbling structure—for which I was supposed to be thankful.

He left me with bad ties across the city. Deals he never made good on. Now, there'd be even more backlash because his final days had been spent bringing vengeful closure to old disputes and seeking catharsis by laying waste to everyone who'd ever wronged him.

Why couldn't he take those last days to make amends? He should've been spending time with his family—with his grandchildren. He should've been leaving them with trust funds and fond memories rather than targets on their backs.

I drove up from the city this evening to meet him in the Cooperstown home. I'd just finished one of his jobs and couldn't go home to Valerie and the kids on account of the blood under my fingernails. Dad laughed the first time I got blood on my hands; he said I was a chip off the old block. He'd left the room whistling, while I cried wondering what kind of man I'd become. His line of work never interested me. In fact, I found it appalling, and I never would've gotten involved if I hadn't absolutely needed to. It'd been a long time coming, and I was ready to relieve myself of the burden, to stand up to him, tell him how I feel, and end the violence in my life. For the kids and Valerie…and for myself. After I washed off the blood from today's job, I knew it would be my last. There was no fucking way I'd take over his business. And he couldn't do anything about it.

He'd been laid up here for weeks, and his doctor said he didn't have much time. Myocardial infarction necrosis is what they called it. Each heart attack killed cells within the heart, increasing the chances for another. I pictured a blackened patch of dead tissue spreading outward, eager to claim pink muscle and flesh, laying ruin to all it touched. He'd had more episodes than we all could count at this point, but Dad's heart was a necrotic clump of putrid rot even before his first heart attack.

Mom said that I got my anger issues from him. Maybe I wouldn't have been so fucking angry all the time if he wasn't my father. Some kids grew up hearing arguments behind closed doors. I grew up hearing gunshots and bodies drop.

Despite all this pent-up anger, despite all the people I've killed on his behalf, there was only one person I've ever truly hated.

But as I stared at him this night lying in a queen-sized bed with an unconnected heart monitor by his side, all I could feel was pity for him. This was how I knew I would never be my father—how I knew I was a better man than him in every way.

"I forgive you," My whispered words shriveled into silence. I wasn't sure I believed them. I passed fully through the strips of plastic into his bedroom office. Dad had insisted on hospice care at home, fearful someone might have tried to gun him down in the hospital. So, he'd hired some medical staff to turn his bedroom into a makeshift clean room. Plastic sheets covered the walls around him. His chestnut desk sat only a few feet away, so he could still work from home while receiving care. Mom had said that the on-call nurse was staying at a motel five minutes down the road. She was to stay off the premises, except for checking daily vitals and for any emergencies that may have arisen.

Being in the same room with him set me on edge. It had always felt that way, but it was different this time. Dad was a virus, and everything he touched went bad. The toxic air expelled from his rotting insides lingered in the air I breathed. The acrid tinge of evil slithered inside, swirled in my belly and conjured that raged I'd been trying so hard to keep buried.

I closed my eyes and quelled the rising hatred. When I opened them, Dad had shot to an upright position in bed. Blue moonlight glinted off a suppressor at the end of his Nighthawk pistol. His finger was ready on the trigger, but he hesitated.

"You should know better than to sneak up on a sleeping old man," Dad said, sliding the silenced pistol back under his pillow.

I swallowed the black lump that had climbed to my throat. It wanted to be unleashed on him for pulling a gun on me.

"Just got in a little while ago. Thought I'd check on you."

Dad leaned to get a closer look at his bedside digital alarm clock. "It's midnight. Where's your mother?"

"She went to bed. She said you were—"

"Did you do the job?"

I didn't answer; I wouldn't give him the pleasure of knowing I'd done exactly as he'd asked—as always. Too many years have been spent living in fear of his ever-growing shadow. Too many years as his errand boy.

Just tell him. Be a fucking man and tell him.

Dad swung his feet over the side of the bed and grabbed his chest, lowering his head with a wince.

"Are you okay?" Sometimes, I wished he would hurry up and die already. Get it over with so we could all get on with our lives. Thoughts like these were intrusive fuckers that I'd been working to silence. I pulled in a deep breath to damper the anger.

He held his monitor stand for support as he attached the pulse oximeter to his finger for a reading. The screen beeped to life reading 98% and 130 BPM.

"Is that normal?" I asked

"Strong as a racehorse." His voice cracked.

"Since you're up," I said, voice hardening in

preparation for whatever he might say in retort. "I need to talk to you about something."

"It's late. It can wait 'til morning."

"No, it can't."

Dad's shoulders broadened and his body swelled as if being filled with ammunition, ready to fire at will.

I squared up to him. "It's about your business."

"What about it?" His tone darkened, looming like a storm.

"I'm not sure it's for me."

Dad dropped a hand on my shoulder and squeezed, nostrils flaring. In the failing moonlight, I could see something eclipse his eyes as he fought his initial belligerent reaction. Instead, he clenched his jaw and said, "You're a natural, Danny. You'll do great."

I cringed. "I'm not a natural. Not in any way."

"You're gonna be fine—you're just like me…"

"I'm nothing like you."

Dad laughed. "I used to say that about my father."

"I want out."

"That's not the way this business works." His expression turned to stone. "I told you that three years ago when you came to me for money."

"I know but—"

"There ain't no dipping your toes into this job. Once you're in, you're in."

"I understand, but—"

"But what?" His booming voice silenced me, but only for a moment.

"You're leaving me with a pile of shit to clean up and

I don't want it." It was the first time in my life I'd ever said exactly what I wanted to say to him. Both relief and terror fought for control of my body.

Dad's once-intimidating frame was diminished in his weakened state. Fatigue plagued him and he seemed to give up on the argument. "Go to bed, son. We have a lot to discuss in the morning."

"I won't be here in the morning."

The monitor spiked to 180 BPM and Dad yanked the clip from his finger. "Don't fuck with me, boy."

"I'm not—"

"You can't get out once you have blood on your hands."

"It was a mistake—"

"*All* of those bodies were mistakes?" Dad's lips curled into a sinister grin.

"I mean it was a mistake to work for you. I want a clean start."

"Blood stains don't come clean just by quitting."

"Then what do I have to do?" My voice raised, and even though there was no way Mom would be able to hear it from the other side of the house, I tried to gain control so as not to wake her.

"You *will* take over what I've built for you."

"No. I won't. Valerie and the kids are all that matter to me now."

"You have commitments to this business."

"I have commitments to my wife and kids. This isn't a discussion." With great trepidation, I turned away. Getting all the to the doorway seemed like an impossible span to navigate with his fury building behind me.

"Don't turn your back on me!"

I knew I was right walking away, but I also knew Dad believed with every remnant bit of his decrepit heart that I had wronged him. I heard him shuffling behind, silk pajama pants swishing together between his gaunt thighs.

He grabbed my shoulder and spun me around to face him. Rage filled his eyes and the cool hard suppressor of his Nighthawk pressed into the soft tissue under my chin.

Dad's pupils dilated, fetid with hatred and evil as if the filthy black rot in his heart had bled into his eyes. I grabbed his arm, fighting against the gun. My other hand pressed flat against the plastic-covered wall, clawing for a blunt object—anything I could grasp to fight back.

His vile expression contorted and saliva strung from his lips. "You and your wife wouldn't have kids if it weren't for *my* money. You wouldn't have a home, a job…you'd be worthless." Dad shoved me so hard against the wall the drywall cracked. His finger squeezed dangerously too tight over the trigger.

"I know…" I said, pulse throbbing between my ears. He'd had me shoved against the wall too many times in my life to be scared anymore. A cloud of his hot breath sat on my tongue and my lips curled in disgust. His darkness wanted inside of me, but I couldn't let that happen. I had too much at stake. "I'm done, Dad. It's time for me to walk away."

"Go ahead and leave, son." Dad's tone softened, but the barrel of the gun remained pressed against my chin. "Leave, and I'll take your family with me when I go."

They say you don't know what you're capable of until you're staring down the barrel of a gun, but I'd had too many guns pointed in my face since childhood to understand this phrase. For me, I didn't know what I was capable of until my kids' lives were at stake.

Sure, I'd killed people, but those hits were not out of some uncontrollable inferno within. They were simply jobs. Nothing more.

But now, with this threat, something stirred inside. Something dark and hateful rose like bile from the depths of my gut and into my heart. It pumped through my bloodstream, polluting every cell in my body, demanding I take action.

I forced Dad's gun out from under my chin. He was strong, even in his condition. We struggled, wrestling back and forth in a violent tango for control of the weapon. In the darkness of the room, blood leaked from Dad's eyes as capillaries burst under stress, leaving black streaks along his face. Teeth gnashed and it was clear this time that his intent wasn't just to scare me. I'd denied him his blood-right over my soul, refused to let his evil take over, and there was nothing else he could think to do but to kill me. To stop me from becoming anything but his protégé.

Mid-struggle, Dad's grip on my arm loosened. He released me and clamped his left arm to his body. His fist pressed firmly into his chest. The fingers of his right hand uncurled, barely keeping purchase on the handle of the gun.

Dad staggered to the bedside landline, fumbled for the phone, but dropped the receiver when he tried to pick it up. For a moment, life returned to his bleeding, black eyes. They widened with desperation as he looked to me for help.

I couldn't do anything but watch as Dad collapsed to his knees.

"What's the matter?" I stood over his helpless frail body, feeling a darkness spreading within myself. "Can't make a phone call without your worthless son?"

His expression went cold, refocusing his attention on the dropped receiver.

I examined my father—the infamous Valencio Ballenger—now withered and sullen.

"What am I worth to you now?" I asked.

His body lacked the vitality to fight as his heart seized. But I didn't trust he wouldn't try. I snagged a corner of sheet plastic from the wall and tore it from the ceiling. With a swift fling of the material, it draped over his head. Dad struggled beneath—a pathetic attempt to thrash. The corded receiver worked well wrapped around his body to keep him from squirming out of the plastic.

All I had to do was wait for his decaying heart to quit, or for his dwindling air supply to give out, and I would finally be through with his tyranny. There was something pleasing about watching him struggle for air. Something terrifyingly delightful to witness his suffering.

I was ready when his right arm raised hastily, gun in hand. My quick deflection forced the barrel back onto himself. Dad pulled the trigger a half-second too late and it fired. The suppressor muffled the gunshot as the bullet launched upward through his lower jaw and out the top of his head. The loose bulge of plastic over his head caught nearly all the blood splatter from spewing across the room.

Moonlight spilled through the window, illuminating his blood-draped face beneath the thick layer of plastic. Dad fell over.

It was too easy. He couldn't be dead yet. A man like him doesn't fall without a bigger fight. I placed the pulse oximeter on his left forefinger and waited for the numbers to beep…beep…beep… slowly declining to zero.

As Dad's diseased heart stopped pumping, the raven-black blood flowing from his head slowed.

He shouldn't have gotten off that easy. My fury was fresh and wanted more blood spilled. More suffering. He deserved decades of torture after what he'd put our family through.

"Fuck you!" I kicked at his head, boot thudding against his skull. I kicked again and again. But no amount of kicking would ever be enough.

I stopped only for a moment before raising my foot and bringing it down with a stomp. "Fuck you!" I screamed chanting, "fuck you, fuck you, fuck you…" each time bringing my boot down onto his head. My spit flung and tears fell. And my hatred for him grew with every crunch of bone that snapped underfoot. A deluge of despair and rage poured out of me. Each crack and snap compromised his skull further until it broke open and my boot sank into his head. The plastic sheet tore on the jagged edge of bone, and bits of blood and brain matter tried to squeeze free from underneath.

I panted in the light of the moon, allowing my pulse to return to normal. The darkness within receeded and I was finally out from under his corruption. Relief washed over me as I realized I would never have to become a hateful monster like my father. Rage evaporated, and a feeling of peace replaced it. A fresh start was in my future.

The corners of my lips twitched into a grin as Dad lay plastic-wrapped in a pool of his own necrotic heart's blood. And not a single drop was on my hands.

HOLLOWED HEARTS

If Wesley could fly out of the school bus window without crashing to his gravel-coated death, he would. He'd stick his torso outside, spread his arms, and let the wind carry him into the sky. He could be like the birds. Take to the clouds, high above the world of problems, and be free from it all. Free from the bullies. Free from the sixth-grade math homework he didn't understand. Free from the embarrassment of not understanding who he was supposed to be.

Wesley pretended not to hear the whispering girls in the seat next to him. How he smelled bad. How his clothes were dirty and that he'd worn the same shirt yesterday. Maybe it was true. He didn't always think about things like that. Sometimes Wesley forgot to shower, and often the cleanest clothes he had were the ones on his back.

Mom and he had moved into the house on Palmer Street a week ago, and Mom swore up and down that Wesley would be happier here. The neighborhood was nicer, but their house was the smallest on the street. Only a two-bedroom ranch, surrounded by Cape Cods and even a couple Victorian-style homes, like the abandoned one across the street. It towered over their tiny house like a peacock with a full plume, flaunting its greatness. The way Casey Phillips in the seat beside him liked to brag about having the latest phone and the most expensive clothes.

Her whispers crawled into his brain and ate away at what little confidence he had. When the bus finally stopped at his corner, he and ten other students filed out, including Casey and her best friend. Casey's straight black hair was parted perfectly without a strand out of place, flowing over her shoulders like a stream of black ink—clean, precise. In the reflection of the school bus door, Wesley's hair was curly and untamed, he couldn't remember the last time he'd tried to comb it. Mom used to make him do all that stuff, but since she got her new job, she didn't have time anymore. Maybe he needed to start taking care of himself now that he was entering manhood. At least, that's what all the boys were saying in their family-living course at school. Soon, he'd be sprouting hair in the craziest places. He turned his nose toward his shoulder and sniffed to verify his armpits had already turned to onions. Casey and her friend were right about the smell.

He wanted to speak up for himself and explain, but it would only make things worse. Instead, Wesley kept his eyes on his feet as he headed home, while the girls walked the opposite direction over the railroad tracks toward the nicer neighborhood with the greener yards and newer houses.

"He lives across the street from Scary Larry," Casey said before he'd gotten out of earshot. Wesley turned to look at the girls. They giggled, grabbing each other's arms and hurried away.

Rumors of Scary Larry were everywhere in this town. Some of the kids called him Hairy Larry. He was an old man who lost his mind and killed himself in the peacock Victorian house across the street from him, but that's all Wesley knew because it'd happened prior to Wesley moving in.

With hands deep in his pockets, walking the concrete gutter at the edge of his street without sidewalks, he neared his house. Rickety wooden steps—Mom called it a porch, but it was no more than two steps as wide as the doorway—creaked underfoot, and Wesley hesitated before letting himself inside with his key. It was always lonely coming home after school. Mom would be home by seven, but for those few hours, all he could do was sit in his room and struggle through homework he couldn't figure out. If he had a friend, or maybe if someone would give him a chance at being a friend, he'd go to their place and hang out, playing video games and eating junk food, or whatever friends do. But all Wesley had was himself, and his home was about as welcoming as a wet sock.

He turned to face Scary Larry's old home across the street, admiring the turret with a spike sticking out of the top. It boasted a full porch painted in teal and coral, with a covered roof and posts and everything porches were supposed to have. Unlike his busted little steps only wide enough for one and a half butts to sit upon.

He sat on them anyway and worked on his homework the best he could. He must have been there for at least an hour or two, mostly dreaming of living in a big house like the one across from him. Homework was a lost cause as he imagined running up and down the staircase inside Scary Larry's.

The sky was darkening, which meant Mom would be home soon. But as he packed his work into his bag, he caught sight of a black and white cat crouched low at the edge of the property. His back end wiggled, front end low, narrowing its gaze on a prey. Wesley followed its eyes to a small black bird who made tiny hops into the backyard between broken iron bars.

The cat sped after it, disappearing between the rungs of the gate.

"No!" Wesley dropped his backpack and sprinted across the street, determined to keep that mangy old cat from getting the bird. He got to the fence and squeezed between bars, then high-stepped through uncut grass along the side of the house, past the smelly garbage cans, all the way to the back yard. The cat leaped, reaching its claws as the little bird narrowly escaped its deadly clutches. Wesley let out a sigh, relieved the little guy got away.

Thick gray clouds choked out the sunlight. And with the tall pines surrounding Scary Larry's backyard, it may as well have been night already. Overhead, the little black bird flitted across the sky, chaotically. It zig-zagged strangely, unlike most birds he'd seen. Wesley had trouble focusing in the failing light, but when he caught sight of the wings, he quickly identified it as a bat. Another bat fluttered out of the trees. How beautiful they were, silhouettes of black against the oppressive gray clouds above, flapping around in any direction they wished, knowing the world couldn't touch them.

Wesley sat in the overgrown grass, letting the tall, seeded tips tickle the back of his neck. He relaxed on his elbows, sinking below the grass level, as bats zipped from tree to tree, and from bat-house to bat-house. That guy Larry must've installed the wooden houses on every pine lining the yard.

Wesley adjusted his elbow to move away from what he thought was a rock grinding against him. Instead, that hard material digging into his skin was a small white bone. He dug it from the ground and noticed there were several more bones surrounding it. A full skeleton in pieces—bat bones with long finger-like wings. He pushed himself from the earth and scanned the ground between the grasses to find scattered bat skeletons all over the yard.

As he backstepped away from the bones, his heel caught on the edge of something hard, and he stumbled. A basement entryway swallowed him whole and Wesley tumbled down a set of stone steps, crashing onto an unforgiving dirt floor. The stench of ammonia filled his nose and he gagged as he rose to his feet. Scant illumination from the failing daylight reached only a few feet into the cavernous basement, but it revealed enough. Hundreds of bats hung from the exposed beams overhead.

Wesley ran up the steps, almost tripping again on his way out. Around the side of the house, heading back toward the fence, he crashed into a garbage can, knocking it over. Wesley made it to the fence, but then paused.

"Calm down!" He rolled his eyes at himself for being such a chicken. There was no need to panic over nothing but a bunch of bats. And he certainly didn't want to get in trouble for knocking over the trash, so he took a breath and walked back to pick it up.

The black bin lifted upright with ease, but the lid had popped open. Tiny, furry dead things dropped out with a percussion of meaty thuds upon the earth. Wesley gasped, cupping his hand over his mouth at the sight of at least a dozen tiny bat carcasses. Maggots rained down with the bodies, squirming in blackened wounds. Each bat had varying levels of decay, but all had the same injury—a hole in its chest.

This time, Wesley let the panic control him, he shot away from the scene as fast as his feet could take him. He squeezed his body between the bars and scurried across the street, where his mom's car was in the driveway.

"Young man," a strange woman's voice said. "What were you doing back there?" Wesley turned as he reached his house. One of the neighbors closed her car door and headed toward him. "It's not safe."

Wesley's mom opened the front door. "Hey kiddo!" She opened her arms for a hug but he bypassed her and ran around the corner into the hall as the neighbor's voice came more clearly into earshot. She stood at the front door with Mom, while Wesley hid out of sight.

"Just letting you know—I know you're new to the neighborhood—that property where your boy was playing is infested with bats."

Wesley's heart thundered in his chest. The stench of ammonia and rotten bat flesh clung to the inside of his nostrils.

"Oh! Good to know," Mom said.

Wesley peeked around the corner and down the hallway to see the neighbor standing outside.

Mom's hand was on the doorknob, ready to close it. "I'll let him know not to go over there."

"I'm Gina."

Mom extended a hand. "Rachel."

"The city really needs to do something about all those bats. That old man that lived there before used to feed them and lure them in. Now he's dead and the bats won't go away."

"I'm sorry to hear that."

The neighbor leaned in, checking over her shoulder before speaking as if someone on the street might be listening. She clutched a necklace between her fingers. "My cousin was his caretaker. It's a very sad story. He wasn't right in the head. Dementia or Old Timer's or something…"

"That is sad. I had a grandfather with Alzheim—"

"He jumped from the top of his roof." Gina interrupted, turning around to point. "Did a swan dive from that turret."

"Oh my God."

"That's not the worst of it! He thought he could *be* like the bats. My cousin used to stop in once a day to check on him. One day, he found him over there with dead bats on the table…" Her voice lowered, nearly inaudible from Wesley's vantage point. "…eating their hearts."

"Sounds like he needed more extensive care than just a once-a-day visit. It's a shame—"

"Trent was so freaked out—Trent's my cousin—he called the police. But when he told Larry the cops were coming, Larry ran upstairs. My cousin didn't know… he didn't know he could climb up on the roof… terrible thing."

"Jesus." Mom said. "Makes you wonder what was happening in his head."

Wesley pictured the garbage can full of heartless bats. The sound of their lifeless bodies falling to the ground, *thud thud thud*… beating in his ears. A morbid dance of sound and stench as fresh as it was moments ago.

Gina sighed, shaking her head. "Larry used to be some important scientist or something. But then his brain got all mixed up."

"It's a vicious disease that hurts more than just the person inflicted," Mom said. She looked over her shoulder.

Wesley ducked out of sight, but she made eye contact with him before he could disappear into his room. He pulled open his curtain, exposing a view of Larry's house. Mom and Gina continued to talk for a few minutes, but he couldn't make out what they were saying.

Things went silent and Gina headed home. Moments later, his bedroom door opened.

"Hey kiddo," Mom said. "How was school?"

Wesley shrugged. He stopped telling her how hard it was weeks ago. She'd kept telling him that "*life is hard, sometimes we just have to suck it up.*" Wesley had been trying to suck it up, but every time he did, he just sucked in another breath. Breaths that kept building up, and he could never seem to ever release them. He was so full of all the sucking-it-up, he could burst.

She sat on the bed beside him, making an effort to be a good mom, but he knew she'd be walking away in a minute to cook dinner and ignore him for the rest of the night.

"Love you." She kissed him on the forehead and stood up. "I'll go get dinner started… mac and cheese, okay?"

He nodded. "I saw the dead bats back there."

"You didn't touch them, did you?" Mom's eyes widened. "Go wash your hands."

"I saw the bats…" Wesley tried to remember if he had touched one when they spilled out of the can, but he couldn't recall. Was that sensation on his hand the touch of the can, of the bone he'd plucked from the ground, or had one of the bloodied furry bodies landed on him?

"Bats carry rabies and other gross diseases. Go wash your hands, now." Mom pointed. "Actually… you haven't showered lately, have you?"

After he scrubbed his hands and showered, Wesley moseyed into the kitchen and scooped out a large helping of blue-box macaroni and cheese—his favorite. Mom cooked actual meals sometimes, like when she could get off work early enough. But most nights it was ten-minute-dinner night, as she liked to call it.

Mom sat in front of the TV with a glass of wine and a bag of chips, feet up.

"Do you want to play a game tonight?" Wesley asked.

Mom smiled. "Awww…. I do. But I'm so tired. I was just going to finish this show and go to bed early. Maybe tomorrow?"

He nodded. It was always *maybe tomorrow* with Mom. He was certain she meant well. She anticipated she'd have the energy to spend on him, but then tomorrow would come and—yet again—Wesley's mom had already spent it all.

"Goodnight, kiddo!"

Wesley turned away.

"Love you!" Mom's eyes stayed on the television screen.

Wesley glanced back and mumbled the sentiment in return, heading to his room.

He sat on his bed, trying to decide what to do. He was bored of his games. Bored with reading. Bored with his room and the toys he'd outgrown. It was pretty pathetic his only friend in the world was his mom and he had to beg for her time.

Wesley stared out his window at the big Victorian home with the colorful porch, wondering if the bats lived in the whole house, or if they were confined to the basement. With hands folded under his chin, resting on the windowsill, he dreamed of the bats inside and wondered if Mr. Scary Larry used to walk around the house with them hanging over his head. Like a crazy cat lady, maybe Larry just loved bats…loved them so much he ingested their hearts. Gobbled them up, just like Mom used to say she could do to Wesley back when he was much smaller.

"I love you so much, I could just gobble you up!"

The only thing Wesley loved was his mom, but eating her heart would be nasty. His face went sour at the thought, and he drew his eyes to the clouded sky. Sporadic bat sightings fluttered as silhouettes against the clouds.

But then movement from the attic window drew his attention. From that tall window under the turret, several bats burst out at once, scattering across the sky. This conjured a smile and he cupped his hands around his face to reduce the glare of his bedroom window. Following the exodus of bats, a figure appeared in the window. A ghostly gray shape against the black grew within the frame, until Wesley was certain it was looking right at him. He sank away from the glass without losing sight of the figure.

With the light off in his room, maybe he couldn't be seen. From the window under the turret, a person's arm reached outside. One with long and spindly fingers that clung to the side of the house. It was a man up there. He pulled himself onto the ledge, crouched like a gargoyle in the open frame, then he twisted around and scaled the side of the house. He scrabbled up the steep roof, a black blur of a figure against the bruised sky.

"Larry?" Wesley whispered to himself.

The figure stopped abruptly, turning to face Wesley's house. He couldn't make out features of the man's face, but Wesley was certain he was looking right at him. Larry went back to climbing the roof, until he was at the tippy top of tallest turret, clinging to the spiky pole.

Wesley didn't want the man to hurt himself, so he tore out of his room, yelling for his mom to call for help. He opened the front door, running barefoot into his front yard where Larry—or whoever it was—had stretched his arms out to the sides, preparing to jump.

Wesley froze. He didn't shout *No* or *Stop* or anything that he should've said. He simply watched as Larry spread his wings, ready to make a dive to his death…again.

However, when Larry was at the highest point of his jump, he brought his arms to his sides, and instead of gravity pulling him to the earth, he zipped up into the sky, disappearing behind thick clouds.

Mom chased Wesley outside, but she missed it.

"What are you doing?" She placed her hand on Wesley's back, guiding him into the house. "You nearly gave me a heart attack!"

"I thought I saw…" He looked over his shoulder at the sky over the turret, waiting to see if Scary Larry would come crashing down, but he never did.

Why bats? Wesley asked himself all day at school. He normally couldn't concentrate anyway, mind always muddied with other nonsense. But today's distraction was important. The teacher jostled his brain back to task, inciting laughter in the class when she said, "Earth to Wesley…"

Great. Just what he needed. More kids laughing at him. At least today he was clean, with fresh-from-the-wash clothes. But that didn't matter much. The kids at school had already made up their minds about him. From this point on, it didn't matter if he was the richest, cleanest kid in school, he'd forever be branded the dirty, smelly kid. And the kid who wasn't very smart.

While the class continued their lesson, he let his mind drift back to the bats. Why not be a bird—a beautiful, feathered bird with colors brighter than the porch of Larry's house? Why'd Larry choose disease-ridden, hairy, scary bats? All Wesley could figure was that bats were closer to people than birds, being mammals and all. And if Scary Larry was some scientist before, maybe he was onto something.

The questions followed him all day. He wondered if he'd really seen Scary Larry—or the ghost of him—fly into the sky. Maybe Wesley was just tired like Mom had said. Or maybe there was something real about what had happened. His curiosity devoured him. Even at lunch, he had trouble focusing on eating because of all the questions and uncertainty. The only thing that brought his attention back to reality were the snickering kids in the cafeteria who had pulled the chairs at their tables away from Wesley, acting like he was some untouchable thing—like some disease-ridden bat.

On the bus ride home, Wesley sat alone again. His head leaned against the glass of the window, eyes brimming with tears, but he refused to let them fall. He willed his eyes to dry up, to choke back the tears and *suck it up* even if it meant he drowned himself in the process. Casey and her friend sat behind him today, talking about their phones and shopping with their parents. The bus was loud and raucous with the excitement of going home on a Friday after school.

A kid in the seat ahead of him turned around. "Hey. Don't you live across the street from Scary Larry's?" The kid was tall, and looked much older. He had to have been in the eighth grade.

Wesley nodded.

"Cool…"

Another guy popped up in the seat beside him. "Can you see the blood stain?"

Wesley's internal alarms were screaming as two older boys asked him questions. He wanted to shrivel inside of himself and hide, but he just sat there, staring with wide eyes, unsure what to say.

The first guy elbowed his friend. "Did they really need a shovel to scrape him off the pavement?"

The friend cringed and laughed.

"Hey kid! I'm talking to you."

Wesley turned his head from them, looking out the window, hoping the boys would just disappear, because he knew any minute, they'd find something to bully him about.

"Whatever…" the boy said.

Wesley tried to block them out, but more voices chimed in. They were low, hushed tones, but he heard them clearly despite the racket of the bus noise.

"He's new."

"So weird."

"…smells…"

Laughter followed and Wesley sank into his seat, ignoring them all.

The bus finally rolled to his stop and he filed out with

the other kids. This time, Casey and her best friend did not go to their neighborhood across the tracks. They followed him down his street.

Wesley looked back frequently. When he did, they'd pretend to look over their shoulders, nonchalantly. When he neared his house, he stopped and faced them.

"What?" Casey asked.

"Don't you live that way?" Wesley pointed toward the rich neighborhood. His heart could've jumped from his chest from the confrontation alone.

"It's a free country!" her friend said.

Wesley walked toward his house.

"Oh my god, he really does live right next to it." Casey grabbed her friend's shirt sleeve and tugged. "Ewww."

He unlocked the door.

"I think I'd die if I had to live in a house that small…" Casey and her friend stood outside for a few seconds and then turned back toward their own neighborhood.

Wesley dropped his bag. The cold dark of his house engulfed him, offering no comfort. Offering no embrace to keep him safe from the world out there. His mom was normally home early on Fridays, but not today. He pulled his flip phone from his backpack—he never took the ancient piece of technology out of the bag in front of other people—and he checked the message from his mom.

Hey, kiddo. I have to work a double. Leftover mac and cheese in the fridge.

Maybe we can play that game tomorrow.

Wesley set the phone on the counter and stood alone in the kitchen. *Tomorrow.*

He was sure what would happen. It would be Saturday, and Mom would need to catch up on housework and yardwork. She'd have him help, but mostly she'd get stressed out that there wasn't enough time to get everything done. By the end of the day, she'd be exhausted. Always exhausted. Always looking to spend time with him tomorrow, but never today. But Wesley knew deep down that the tomorrow he dreamed of—the one where he and Mom had fun playing games and going out to dinner—*that* tomorrow would never come.

Wesley would always be the untouchable boy. He'd never have anyone to look up to other than the birds—and the bats—in the sky.

Drawn to the house across the street, he gazed at the attic window where he'd seen the man last night. Everyone said Scary Larry had jumped to his death, but Wesley knew the real story.

Wesley knew Larry's secret.

Before he realized what he was doing, he stepped out of his house and crossed the street to Larry's front yard. From the ground, the tallest turret seemed to stab the sky, piercing a hole right through it. Like it could create a portal to another world—a world up there with the bats and the birds.

Larry's front door creaked open as if welcoming him inside.

Wesley accepted the offer and stepped over the threshold, closing the door behind him.

Inside, the scent of ammonia hit him, but he spotted no bats hanging from the ceiling, nor flitting around the room. The odor from the basement must've wafted up the steps and into the foyer. Straight ahead, a staircase led to the second floor. As much as he wanted to run up and slide down the banister, Wesley couldn't resist entering the dining room.

A large formal table had eight chairs neatly placed on all sides. At the head of the table, sat a clean white plate with a small bat, wings splayed. Beside it, a crisp, folded napkin with a fork and a sharp knife.

As dusty as the place was, Wesley was pleased to see the dining table was buffed to a shine, as if someone had been taking care of it. He sat at the head of the table and pulled his chair in, poking the small bat with his fingertip. It was soft and fleshy, without a foul odor, so it couldn't have been dead for long.

Was he supposed to eat it? *Gross!*

Why would Larry offer this to him? Wesley prodded the bat with the prongs of his fork and then checked over his shoulders to see if anyone was watching. Like Casey was going to pop out from behind a door and take pictures of him sitting here.

Part of him didn't care. If people were going to talk about him anyway, make fun of him no matter what, what would it matter if he stuck his fork into this bat and gobbled it up?

It had to be a delicacy in some country, somewhere, *right*?

Wesley figured it was no different than doing a dissection in science lab—not that he'd done that in school yet. But he'd watched enough videos online to figure it out. He poked the tip of the knife into the bat's chest. It pierced the skin with a pop, then sliced through with ease. Much smoother than the dull knives from his house. Flesh tugged momentarily, blade scraping ribs. The fur and skin had been cut away, exposing bone and sinew and a dark burgundy heart. Wesley pinched his fingers around the ribcage and pried the bones back. They cracked like dried twigs. He used the knife again to cut the tiny heart free from vessels holding it in place, then held the bloody knotted piece of tissue in the palm of his hand.

Such a perfect little organ. No bigger than a peanut M&M. Wesley looked over his shoulder again, but this time two bats flitted by, zooming over the stairs up to the second floor and out of sight. The flapping of their wings on the air and the freedom of their existence brought a smile to Wesley's face. To be like them would be perfection.

And he *could* be like them. He'd seen what had happened to Larry—he didn't fall to his demise. *No!* He did the opposite. He rose above up into the clouds.

So, Wesley popped the heart into his mouth like he would a piece of candy. The muscly tissue rolled over his tongue. The taste of blood made his salivary glands kick in, filling his mouth with blood-tinged spit. His teeth trapped the tiny heart between them, and he slowly bit down, grinding the tough meat between molars until it split in two pieces.

It didn't taste very good, but like Mom said about Brussel sprouts: the benefit would come tomorrow. Maybe if he ate enough, he could absorb their essence and be like the bats. Maybe their hearts held the key to his future. A future that took him off the ground, away from the dirt and grime of his existence. He wouldn't have to bother his mom anymore about playing a game tomorrow. Because tomorrow, he would climb to the tallest turret and fly away from it all.

DON'T MAKE IT WEIRD

A girl is playing football?

Hannah had heard it so many times, it didn't matter who said it anymore. It played in her head like a glitchy recording, over and over on the bus to summer camp in anticipation of whichever boy would say it this year.

"Yeah, a girl is playing football!" She'd puff out her chest to make herself bigger than she really was, but it never mattered. No matter how often she played, how good she got, they never believed that a girl could play. They'd make snide comments or get frustrated when they were stuck with her on their team, but she always proved them wrong.

She was better at communicating through competitive sports, anyway. An interception here. A fake-out spin and redirection there. But every game she played, especially as she got older—now thirteen—it was always the same. She'd play hard. Prove them wrong. And the next game, she'd have to do it all over again. But last year, it got even worse. That's the year her breasts started coming in.

Her bus passed the sign for the camp entrance and Hannah took a deep breath, remembering the trauma of last year. What mom called "nubbins" had appeared just before she left for summer camp. *Breast buds*, according to the doctor. What a stupid name. *Buds*. Like her boobs-to-be were some flowering plant, waiting to be plucked or pollinated or something. Surely a boy invented that term. On the field, the boys treated her like a porcelain doll. They wouldn't touch her. Wouldn't tackle her. They laughed and whispered about her *boobies* as if she wasn't right there, listening, being shaped and molded by every word. What terrible things did they think would happen if they played ball while breasts were on the field?

It was the worst year at camp ever. She'd gone home crying, wishing she didn't have the body parts at all. All she wanted to do was play as an equal. The mirror had reflected her ridiculous nubbins back at her and she cursed them.

"Why can't you be useful!" She wished they'd go away, but more than anything, she wished the boys would shut up. She imagined grabbing a boy—any boy—by the throat and choking him until he went unconscious, and that rage scared her. Violence wasn't a reaction she'd ever given into. Hannah concealed all those bad feelings in a held breath and only dared to release them on the field.

The sore, aching nubbins had been tormenting her. Mom said it was just growing pains, so Hannah tried to ignore it, but they swelled and shifted. Like all her anger and pent-up frustration with the unfairness of it all writhed under her skin, metastasizing within.

She had developed into a C-cup since then. The rapid growth left marks across her chest. Cracks—like the lines her mom had around her cleavage, but these lines were scattered across her breasts. They were scar-like and sensitive.

Mom said they were stretch marks, that her body was blossoming—*seriously, what's with the flower metaphors?*—but Hannah felt like it was something more sinister. Not a blossoming, but an awakening.

"Don't let them own you," her sister Meghan said, as she caught Hannah scolding herself in the mirror. Meghan got them a couple of years ago, and they changed the way everyone looked at her. Suddenly, her nerdy sister had boys flirting with her. Grown men would shoot side glances or double-takes—*Eew.* Hannah wanted none of it.

"You own them." Meghan puffed out her chest, showcasing her cleavage. "You're in charge. Own them."

Her memories of the year prior faded as the camp bus entered the parking lot. The other kids shouted and sang songs—a conglomeration of excitement to swim in the river, paint birdhouses, or play tug-of-war. But Hannah sat silently in her seat, wondering if this year would be a repeat of last. Wondering if people would chastise her for wanting to play football. Wondering if it would be eight thousand times worse because her boobs were eight thousand times bigger.

After orientation and cabin assignments, Hannah quickly found the football field, where a handful of boys had already gathered, planning teams.

The sun was high in the late afternoon sky. The grass smelled freshly mowed. When her feet touched the field, she felt at home. She felt she belonged here… at least until other people told her she didn't.

Two young men in counselor shirts stood at the sideline, talking to each other. None of the boys looked familiar, which meant Hannah had to, yet again, prove her worthiness to play.

Boys get to walk on the field as equals, like they are magically endowed with athletic ability. But when a girl steps up to play, she must prove her worthiness to handle the great pigskin idol.

One boy, blonde hair and ice blue eyes, nodded toward the east buildings. "Arts and crafts are over there."

"Not really my thing. Can I play?"

The boy with blonde hair smirked. "This isn't two-hand-touch—"

"We tackle," another boy said.

"Okay," Hannah said. "I play tackle."

The blonde kid adjusted the football in his grip. "I doubt that."

"No. I can."

"Sorry. Our teams are filled."

A counselor jogged onto the field. Dark, shaggy hair swept to one side. Sparse facial hair covered his jaw. His nametag read *Hunter*. "Travis, what's going on?"

Travis pointed. "*She* wants to play, but it's tackle."

"Hey, sweetheart," Hunter said. "These guys get rough—"

"I know. I'm allowed to play. I was here last year."

Hannah sought out a familiar face to vouch for her, but there was nobody she recognized. "I can play." She stood tall, shoulders broad, trying to square herself off to look tougher. Her chest stuck out as well, but she did her best to own them, like her sister had taught her.

The counselor Hunter shrugged. "Guys, you can't leave any camper out. Those are the rules."

His eyes wandered to Hannah's shirt, which was a bit too small, stretching over her chest. "How old are you sweetheart?"

"Thirteen."

"Jesus…" he turned away and walked toward the sideline.

The second counselor doubled over, laughing. "Were you about to hit on a thirteen-year-old?"

"Shut up… she doesn't look thirteen."

"But you were looking." He covered his mouth, failing to hide his laughter.

Hannah knew that every boy on the field heard those clowns loud and clear. She fought the emotions stirring in her heart. The embarrassment, the anger… She wanted to scream at them, tell them all to shut up, but if she lost her temper, they'd say *"girls are too emotional to play."* So, she buried it deep in her chest. Let it stew there. Let it simmer. Soon, they'd know who they were dealing with. Her breasts ached and a shifting of flesh inside made her cross her arms over herself.

"I guess she has to play…" Travis said.

"This makes it weird." A scrawny kid with red hair made a sour face.

"Why?" she asked.

"Because you're a girl."

"How is that weird?" Hannah put her hands on her hips.

"What if we accidentally touch… something."

"Now *you're* making it weird."

"Whatever …"

"You're on *their* team." Travis nodded across the fifty-yard line at the group of boys. Some of them groaned.

"You're down a player. So, you get the girl." Travis said, then one corner of his lips twisted upward. "Oh yeah… it's shirts and skins."

A kid on the opposing team nodded toward Hannah. "Y'all are skins."

Hannah's team began removing shirts. Some of them seemed oblivious to the situation. Some snickered among each other, watching, waiting to see what she'd do.

"Come on!" she said.

"Oh," Travis said with an arched eyebrow. "They wanna play with the boys until they have to play *like* the boys." Travis cocked his arm back and threw the ball toward her without warning, but Hannah's reflexes were ready. She caught it, cradling it into her chest as it spiraled into her breastbone with a thud.

There was an uproar among the boys on her team, pointing and laughing at Trevor, while Hannah stood her ground with the football in one hand.

"Our team is shirts," she said.

Travis turned away. "Teams are picked. Either take it off like a boy or go home."

A guy on the shirts team with dark hair and glasses was sheepish in his approach toward Hannah, keeping his eyes on his feet. "I'll switch teams with you so you don't have to be skins."

She didn't thank him. Maybe if he spoke up and said how stupid everyone was acting… *that* would be worth her appreciation. This kid in glasses looked for the easy way out. A bargain to keep everyone happy.

The game kicked off, and for several plays Travis refused to pass to Hannah even though she was wide open. She was close to the end zone and well within passing distance—even for Travis, who couldn't throw worth a crap—but not once did he pass her the ball. Rage stirred within, and her chest burned as if a fire were stoking inside. Something churned and coiled under her skin. Hannah ignored the sensation and focused on getting her hands on that ball.

The ball finally turned over to the other team. Defense. Historically speaking, defense was the only time she got to prove herself as a good player because she didn't have to rely on anyone passing her the ball. Defense was where she could showcase her talent. She tore down the field toward a shirtless receiver and leapt in the path of the spiraling ball. Her fingertips reached as far as she could, knocking it away.

Some of the boys shouted with excitement. Others laughed at their friend for being blocked by a girl. One kid tried to argue interference, but everyone saw what happened. There's always one person on the field who has to lie in an attempt to save his masculinity from the utter embarrassment of a girl jumping higher than him.

Hannah got back on the line of scrimmage. She cut down the field, sprinting as fast as her legs could muscle forward. Her brain was like a mathematician, calculating the quarterback's movements and the intended receiver's speed… she knew exactly where the ball was going and she put herself in its path. Hannah scooped it into her arms for an interception. Some of the boys howled and laughed, but Hannah took off in a sprint toward the other end, leaving them behind.

"Get her!"

"Stop her!"

Tunnel vision ahead, she refused to look back and slow her pace. She closed on the endzone but felt someone coming from behind. Hannah pushed harder, but she knew she was about to go down. A hand swiped the back of her leg, then a grip around her ankle sent her crashing into the grass. She landed chest first and the blow crushed her breasts. She felt a pop. Similar to that release of pressure when fingers squeeze a zit and the skin ruptures, releasing a white glob of gunk. She worried if she looked down, she'd see one of her breast scars busted open, spilling glandular goo all over the field. Fortunately, they were still intact.

However, far worse than she imagined, she couldn't breathe. No air would draw into her lungs.

"What's wrong with her?"

Hannah was upright on her knees, looking to the electric blue sky, willing her lungs to pull in some air, but nothing would come.

The counselor's voice came next. "She got the wind knocked out of her."

"Put your head between your knees!" someone said.

Hannah did as she was told and the breath finally came.

Shaken, but not defeated, she dusted off her knees and got to her feet.

The counselor insisted she go to the infirmary, but when Hannah refused, he ejected her from the game.

"But I'm fine now. I can keep playing."

"Those are the rules. Injured players go to the infirmary."

Hannah let out a frustrated sigh. "Fine."

"This game is kind of hardcore," Hunter said.

"That's what makes it fun."

"That's what makes it for boys. Sorry kid, go rest it off." Hunter placed a hand on her back, maybe too low on her back near the waist of her shorts, and he guided her off the field.

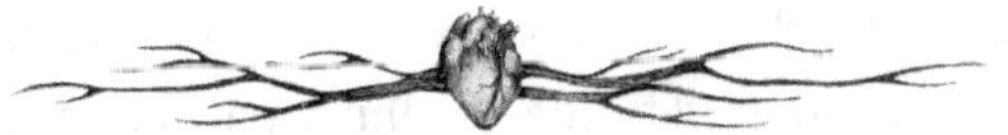

In the shower that evening, she hushed her tears under the cascading water. Her scars stretched, skin undulating. She worried tumors were growing inside, but she didn't want them to become a problem. She couldn't leave after today's incident on the field. Hannah needed another game to show that she was good enough to play. That getting the wind knocked out of you is something that can happen to anyone, and it wouldn't stop her from playing.

She wondered if having breasts made her lose her

breath on impact, and if so, she wasn't about to let them control her life.

"I own you," she whispered. She ran fingers along one of the lines on top, where the tissue had stretched, scar widening. It burned, seering hot, and the skin parted at the seam, flesh strung apart like melted mozzarella. Her whimpers were muffled by running water and hopefully unheard by the other girls in the showers.

She examined the exposed layers of fat and pink underneath the open crevice. Something moved inside. She'd felt it before, squirming just below the skin. A snakelike structure writhed within. With trepidation, Hannah placed a finger into the lacerated skin and touched the thing moving inside, but it retracted. She inserted her finger deeper. A coiled, ropey thing wrapped around her finger and squeezed like a boa constrictor.

Hannah whispered, "Stop," and it released her finger.

It wriggled until an eyeless head emerged with a mouthful of tiny serrated teeth.

Her initial shock and desire to scream were silenced by her fascination with the swelling, pulsing movement within her body.

"Hi," she whispered to the snake thing in her chest.

Back at the cabin, she lay in bed, hiding beneath the covers while the other girls whispered and gossiped among themselves. A knock at the door made all the girls squeal.

"It's a boy! For you, Hannah!" The girls giggled as Hannah jumped from her top bunk and met the kid outside.

The dark-haired boy with glasses, Caleb, stood on the

step. "You okay?"

"I was fine. I could've kept playing."

"Yeah… You're really good," Caleb said.

"Then why didn't you say anything?"

He stared blankly. "You know how it is…"

She waited for him to say something else, to say *how it is*, but there was nothing. He stood there, kicking at the dirt on the steps.

"I don't think you should play tomorrow. Travis is just going to make it harder on you."

"Then I guess I'll make it harder for him, too." Hannah slammed the door in Caleb's face.

Under covers, the snake thing inside curled and pulsated, and for once, it didn't feel wrong. It didn't feel like two alien lumps had taken over her life. No. This thing inside understood Hannah's pain. The aching and inflamed sensation had finally ceased, and she placed her hands on top of her chest while lying on her back. The movement brought her comfort. It undulated like it was breathing in sync with her.

"You're not so bad, are you?"

Hannah crossed the field in the morning wearing shorts and a strappy tank top. Her cleavage was exposed, as were some of her scars. Why should she have to pretend she didn't have them? Why should she cover them up or mash them down just to make boys more comfortable around her?

The counselor, Hunter, let out a slow whistle, just

short of a catcall.

The other counselor, James, reminded him, "Thirteen, man …" He shook his head.

"Doesn't matter when they look like that."

Hannah stepped up to the group of boys.

"We already picked teams, so…" Travis gestured to the sideline.

Hannah counted. "Looks like skins is down a player."

Travis grinned. "You gonna take your shirt off?"

Hannah grabbed the underside of her tank top and slowly lifted, ready to go skins if it meant she could play.

Let them look. If they see a couple of tits in a nonsexual light, maybe they won't be so shocked the next time another girl comes around.

Caleb interjected. "Shirts and skins is stupid anyway."

Travis rolled his eyes. "Whatever. She can be on the skins team and not take her shirt off … she's showing enough skin anyway."

Hannah snarled at him. "You got a problem with my skin?"

The counselor, Hunter, jogged up. "Hannah ..." He dragged his hand through his hair. "Why are you doing this? What are you trying to prove?"

"I'm doing it for the same reason they are… I want to play football. That's it. Is that so hard to understand? Why do I have to *prove* anything?"

"All right," Hunter sighed. "You're asking for whatever happens …"

"Let's just play!" someone shouted.

Her frustration fueled her gameplay again. Hannah

ripped down the field, feet kicking up dirt along the way. She cut to the right so she'd be wide open for a pass. Travis tailed her as the quarterback, for once, actually passed her the ball. Hannah leapt high, snagged the ball with her fingertips, and tucked it tight to her chest as Travis crashed into her. She went down hard, and at least two other boys dog-piled her. While wrestling for the ball—of which she maintained possession the entire time—someone grabbed a handful of her breast. She screamed, which got the boys to climb off of her. One boy pulled away—the scrawny kid with red hair. He held his finger in his mouth, then pulled it away to look at it. Blood oozed to the surface.

She turned her back, checking her breasts as the snake-thing slinked back into her chest. A sly smile crept across her lips and she tried to contain it.

"Thanks, buddy," she whispered to her inner friend. "Look at you being useful." Another snake slithered over the slit. There were *more* inside. Hannah bit her lip to contain her excitement.

"She bit me!" The red-haired kid pointed his bloody finger at her.

"You grabbed me."

Hunter jogged onto the field with a growl. He took a look at the kid's finger. "Dude, go to the infirmary and get that cleaned up. And you…" he pointed to Hannah. "You're out."

"I didn't bite him."

"Then why is he bleeding?"

"I don't know. But a better question would be why did he grope me?"

"You have to sit out."

"No." Hannah ignored Hunter and went to the line of scrimmage, ready for the next play.

Now that the game had uneven players, Caleb volunteered to sit out so Hannah could continue to play. "She's better than me, anyway," he said. A kind gesture, but at this point, Hannah needed the boys on her side to do more than sit on the sideline in approval of her existence on the playing field. She needed them to pass her the ball. She needed them to not accuse her of cheating when she succeeded.

She needed their skin in the game.

On the next play, she was determined to score the touchdown. She sprinted down the field as the quarterback cocked back his arm. Travis grabbed her by the waist to keep her from getting in the open, and she tried to fight him off.

"Holding!" She grunted in his grip.

Not a single boy had her back. Nobody cared that Travis cheated. Hunter stood on the sideline, flirting with one of the older campers.

Hannah kept charging forward, breaking free as the ball left the quarterback's hands. She turned and leapt for the incoming pass, but Travis jumped in front of her to block. The will to win busted through, and the snake things came with it. They split her skin open at all the creases, shooting out like a dozen grappling hooks on fleshy ropes. Shredding tiny holes through her tank top, they lashed out. The snakes bit into Travis's back, all of them at once. His arms flung up as they tore him to the ground, biting, nipping, feasting. Hannah caught the incoming ball. Her hands snagged it overhead and she dropped to the ground in the end zone.

The field was loud with screaming, but her vision was narrowed in on the fleshy monsters as they feasted on Travis. Hannah took a knee and a deep breath, then summoned them back inside. They did as requested, retracted, coiling into her breasts, and sealing the skin with a mucous membrane.

Travis writhed on the ground, bloody wounds peppering his body. He stood, trembling, and then darted off toward the infirmary, spinning to look behind every few seconds.

Hannah turned to face the boys who'd all run in the other direction, except Caleb who remained on the bench paralyzed, jaw hanging open.

Hunter approached slowly, palms up. "What happened? I didn't see…"

Meanwhile, the other counselor James backed off the field and ran away.

"What did you do to him?" Hunter stared off toward Travis, whose blood-splattered body shrunk in the distance.

"Don't you mean, what did *they* do to me?"

"What happened to him? Do you have a weapon?"

"No—"

"I need you to come with me." He placed one hand on her back and one on her shoulder.

She yanked away. "I'm not going anywhere with you."

The counselor's eyes widened as they drifted toward her chest. He stared and Hannah dropped her gaze to see why. Her tank top was filthy with a dozen cave-like holes exposing hundreds of tiny teeth. Biting, drooling, dripping with disdain and vengeance.

Whether Hunter was going to search her for a weapon or be a pervert, she didn't know, but his touch, his gaze… it terrified her. Fear and fury took over, and the inner creatures reacted. They shot out of her, latching onto his body. Muscles in her chest contracted. She adjusted her stance to balance the weight as creatures lifted him off his feet, screaming and flailing.

His body pulled in all directions. The pink, ropey snakes ripped him apart. His shrieks turned to sputtering grunts and then to silence. When Hunter was no more than a shredded pile of flesh, they feasted on his muscles, ripping bits of sinew and meat, taking in sustenance that not only fed the creatures, but fueled Hannah as well.

After her inner friends retreated to the cavity in her chest, Hannah turned to see Caleb still sitting on the sideline, traumatized. Not saying or doing anything, as usual. As she walked by him, he scrambled backward, falling off the bench. She stopped next to him. "This is all your fault."

"My fault?"

"I just wanted to play football…"

Caleb held a shirt in front of himself as a shield.

"… but you *boys* had to go and make it weird."

YOUR ORDER
HAS SHIPPED

CONSUMER ALERT

irst thing in the morning, the laptop's glare assaults Meredith's eyes with blinding light. As the computer loads, she pours a cup of coffee and dumps another can of food into her cat's dish. She should probably wash the crusted plastic bowl today. He hasn't been eating as much lately, and now it seems he hasn't touched his breakfast from yesterday. She clicks her tongue to call him.

"Kitty cat?"

Stubborn thing. Probably hunting a mouse in the back room. She really should get that room cleaned out, but she hasn't mustered the courage to go through her husband's things yet.

The clutter on the stove—unwashed pans, pizza boxes, and who-knows-what-else—obstructs the clock, but Meredith knows it has to be about six o'clock based on the way the faint glow of daylight is fighting through the gap in the curtain.

She sets her coffee beside her computer at the kitchen table. Cold fingers hover over her keyboard as she opens her email. It's been chillier lately—enough to see her breath inside—and the reason she purchased the shaggy fleece robe that she wore this morning.

Her eyes adjust to the glare of the screen. A sadistic and pleasureful start to her day.

Your order has been shipped.

It's the crochet kit she'd ordered yesterday. She'd always wanted to learn how to crochet and now, with all this extra time on her hands, she can.

A sidebar advertisement for novelty lawn gnomes pops up. One gnome is being eaten by a dinosaur. Meredith chuckles and clicks on the link. She'll need this too. Perfect for the garden she'll be planting in the spring. Her daughter Allison would love it.

Click.

Consume.

A cat tree—the kind with multiple tiers and scratching posts—is marked down to thirty dollars from a hundred. She can't pass that up, either. Click. Consume.

A knock at the front door draws her attention away from the screen.

Not now.

The door opens to her daughter Allison's voice. "Mom?" She brings with her a waft of the outside world.

"It's freezing in here!" Allison can't see her over the stacks of boxes and treasures Meredith has stacked in the living room at the front of the house.

The front door shuts, and Meredith stays at her computer as Allison goes to the hall to check the thermostat. The raucous noise of something falling is followed by Allison grunting in frustration. "Damn it, Mom! The heat is out! Did you pay your gas bill?"

Meredith chews her fingernail, waiting for her daughter to come around the corner.

"What is that smell?" Allison emerges into view.

Meredith lifts nose to better inhale the scent, but she doesn't know what Allison is talking about. She closes her laptop before Allison can see what she's doing.

"Are you shopping again?" she asks.

"Just a couple little things."

"Mom." Her daughter's nostrils flare a bit, holding back her misplaced anger. "You're blowing through all of his life insurance money."

"You have your share of his money for college. Don't worry about what I do with mine."

Allison picks up one of the boxes piled between them. They're all over the small one-story home. They lay stacked on the couch. At least twenty brown packages of things she ordered last week. And boxes of things to get rid of, things to go through, and more boxes of things she'd ordered online, but hadn't gotten around to opening yet. Meredith will open them eventually, but for now, she takes pleasure in seeing them stacked there, like presents under a Christmas tree.

"Do you even know what's in these?"

Meredith refuses to answer, but tries to be pleasant. "Want some coffee? Sit down."

"No. I don't want a coffee, and I wouldn't even know *where* to sit. Look at this place."

It has gotten a bit out of control. Piles of boxes are

opened and unopened. Projects and crafts—all the things she imagines will bring her joy—she hasn't done them yet. The chairs are full of clothes. They're all stacked neatly, but it's such a small house. If she could get around to cleaning that back room, maybe there'd be more space. Right now, there's only room for a path from the front door, down the hall to the bathroom, and a path to the kitchen where she sets up her laptop. Every night, she has to climb over the heap of things in the back room to get to the connecting bedroom, so cleaning it out would be helpful.

"I know it's a lot," Meredith defends, "but some are gifts I bought for your cousins and for you, and for—"

"You need to stop buying stuff. We've talked about this again and again. It's out of control." Allison scrunches up her nose. "Seriously! What in God's name is that smell?" Allison draws closer to the front window, moves the packages on the couch out of the way, and sniffs several times. After a few seconds of exploring the underside of cushions, she looks behind the couch. Allison gasps and staggers backward.

"What?" Meredith asks.

Allison whips around. Her eyes fill with tears, glaring at her mother in a way she's never looked at her before. She muscles the couch away from the wall, and squats behind. When she comes out, she's holding the stiffened body of her cat.

Meredith cups her hands over her mouth as Allison cradles the frail corpse in her hands.

"I never should have left Max with you when I went

to school!" She pushes past Meredith toward the kitchen.

Unsure how to help her poor daughter, Meredith remains still and quiet. She chews on her fingernail, and the click of it breaking between her teeth soothes her almost as much as buying new things.

Allison carefully places her beloved cat into a plastic grocery bag. Tears are streaming now from her eyes. With her back to her mother, and facing the backroom, Allison whispers, "Oh my god!"

Bins and boxes are stacked to the ceiling along the walls, with a half-sized heap in the middle. Meredith kept the middle of the room more shallow so she could climb over the things to get to the back bedroom at night. The room didn't seem so bad until now—now that her daughter stared, crying, with her childhood cat dead in her arms.

Meredith's vision blurs with tears and she tries to comfort her daughter. "I'm sorry about Max, sweetie. He *was* really old."

She squares up to her mother, hatred painted in her expression. "You're sick, Mom. I've been telling you for over a year now that if you didn't change, I'd have to call for professional help." Her voice wavers as she tries to suppress more tears. "Dad's medals and awards are going to rot in here. Everything is going to ruin because of you."

"I'm going to clean it up," Meredith says.

"No, you won't." Allison navigates over the mound of things.

Christmas decorations. Clothing that didn't fit and needs to be returned. Opened cardboard boxes with treasures she hasn't gotten around to using. And somewhere beneath it, are her late husband's bins of things. Uniforms, awards, and deployment memorabilia. Family photos and the memories of the way life was, back before she had a big empty void inside.

Allison disappears behind a stack of bins taller than her.

"What are you looking for, sweetie?"

Her daughter returns, fumbling over the heap of possessions with something tucked in her jacket.

"What do you have?"

"Nothing you need," Allison says. Her expression says it all.

"Is it your father's—"

"I'm not taking anything that you *need*." She tucked the secret object under her arm and paused at the kitchen table. "I'm taking this back too." She swipes Meredith's smartphone from the table.

Meredith can't argue. Allison pays for it with the money she makes working nights at the restaurant. Without another word, Meredith allows Allison to leave.

And in her sudden absence, there was her husband, Henry, empty of his life's force. The memory of his flag-draped casket lowering into a rectangular void.

She cries for him, and for Allison, and for the cat. But most of all, she cries for the emptiness inside of her.

Once again, Meredith is alone in her cold, dark home, and the void within expands.

An emptiness so great it courses through her veins, through every cell in her body, until she feels so empty she can't bear it. She paces and tries to shake out the itching inside. She needs to fill herself with something… anything.

It's a hunger, not for food, but for feelings. Feelings of happiness. And the only thing that brings her joy lately are simply her things. Things she loves. Things she wants.

Just *things*.

Meredith sits at the laptop, but the internet won't load. She tries again.

Nothing.

"Come on!"

No connection.

Meredith runs to the back room, and scrambles recklessly over the boxes. She makes it to the router— or where the router normally sits. It's gone, taken by her daughter as punishment.

Her heart could implode with the nervous panic coursing through her body. She needs to buy something now. She needs to fill the void.

She climbs back over her pile of things. The blue lid of a storage bin buckles under her weight and her socked foot sinks into a stack of Henry's uniforms. The black velvet painting of an American flag tears, but it doesn't matter. These things don't mean anything to her anymore. They are the things she already has. Things that once brought her joy, but cannot any longer. They've already been consumed by the void. And the void wants something new. Something more.

Biting at her fingernail, she digs out a pair of scissors from a craft box, then scrabbles over the piles, through the kitchen, to the living room. She opens one of the boxes that came yesterday. First, is a pair of socks with llamas printed on them. Adorable…they're going to be a gift for Allison. She loves llamas. She holds them to her chest and smiles.

Another box. A heavy meat tenderizer shaped like a hippopotamus.

Another box...

Twelve unopened boxes are torn through with the voracity of a starving dog. Each brings a moment of satisfaction, but not enough to quell the hunger. The void inside devours each package.

More—it whispers.

She stops to listen, but realizes the voice must've been in her head.

Meredith crumples as the void inside grows, as her heart swells with all the nothingness.

She's crouched on the floor and bites her middle fingernail. Click, click, as bits of fingernail snap off. She bites it down to the quick—until it hurts.

Surrounded by piles of her purchases, she hugs them close to ward off the chilled air, the voice in her head, and the insatiable hunger within.

But none of it can make her happy.

Consume—it's voice is gritty and commanding.

"I can't." Foggy breath leaves her lips. She gnaws at bloodied nail beds, rocking with hunger pangs.

The doorbell rings—a sound of salvation! Finally a package has arrived that will save her from this rising madness.

Chewed, numb fingers grip the doorknob and she swings open the front door.

A man presents her with a box. He's taller than the last guy. Black hair, clean-cut, with the stiff posture of a mannequin. His face is porcelain-slick, almost unreal. Behind him, the street is barren—the signature brown van is nowhere in sight.

He grins, extending the cardboard box toward her. "This should do it."

Meredith snatches it from the man and hugs it to her body. It's light enough to be another pair of socks. She hopes for something better, but she can't remember what she'd ordered. The door closes on the strange man in brown, and Meredith sits on the floor, sore fingers in a frantic attempt to rip the tape. She clenches her hand into a fist and punches through the tape seal.

Black packing peanuts fill the inside. She'd never seen them in black. Meredith digs through, swishing around the foam pieces to find her prize. The soft black foam against her hand brings a moment of sensory bliss as she awaits her fingers to brush whatever awaits her. The energy rushes up her arm and into her heart. The void within is filled with warmth and satisfaction, and she gasps absorbing the ephemeral moment of joy.

But as she swirls her hand through the box, the feeling evacuates. There is nothing inside but the black packing peanuts.

She flips the top flap down to see where it came from, but there is no label on the box. No address at all.

As she tips the box upside down, a black substance

peels from the packing peanuts. A gritty material like sand, but it holds together like a flock of birds, defying gravity just the same. A tiny black sandstorm rises before her, swirls around her fingers and travels up her arm. Before she has a moment to shake it away, it has vanished, absorbed into her skin.

She rubs at it, rushing to the faucet to rinse it off. Her arm aches. Now her shoulder.

The sandstorm scratches within, she can feel it digging through vessels into her bloodstream.

A vehicle door closes out front, breaking her from the feeling under her flesh. Someone is here. Perhaps another package.

Click. Click. Meredith pulls her finger away from her mouth. She didn't realize she was biting her nails again. The tinge of blood sits on her tongue and lips. A middle fingernail has been chewed away completely. Raw flesh oozes, but it doesn't surprise her. Cold air stings the wound. There's something inside her telling her that this should be wrong—that chewing yourself raw is a problem—but there's another part inside whispering that it is good. And it wants more.

Meredith parts the curtain a crack to see a frail, middle-aged woman—probably not much older than Meredith—walking toward the door. A delivery truck is parked behind her.

Consume—it demands.

Something else is in control of Meredith. She feels herself as a whisper of her own conscious mind, swimming in a vast pool of darkness, trying to stay afloat in a swelling Void. The Void speaks over her, pushing her deep within, as the delivery woman rings the doorbell. Meredith begs herself not to open the door, but she has no power here.

The front door opens, and before the delivery woman has time to react, she is grabbed by her tiny wrist, and dragged into the house. The woman screams, tripping over the heap of opened packages, as Meredith—or the thing that has filled her up—grabs the hippopotamus meat tenderizer. It's heavy in her hand, and without even the slightest attempt to fight the Void's control, Meredith bashes the woman over the head.

In a wave of confusion and surrealism, blood splatters onto the things that can no longer fill her. Bits of brain matter sprays onto her face, onto her clothes, and across the window. Onto the new llama socks. Meredith hovers over the bloody pulp. A metallic tang fills her nose and the Void's mouth waters. She sinks her bloodied, raw fingers into the demolished skull cavity and fills herself with something new.

Meredith loses track of time as she lies in bed after the incident with the delivery woman. It's all a blur in her mind. She's terrified that if she gets out of bed and walks into the living room, everything she imagined had happened would be true. But here in this moment, perhaps she could force herself to believe it was a just a nightmare.

With the setting sun, darkness invades the house, and the Void grows hungry again. It swells within her, eager to take control.

From her bedroom, she hears a quick knock and the sound of the front door swinging open.

"Mom?"

The Void stirs, drawing Meredith to her feet. "No," she whispers to the great emptiness. "Not her."

But the Void defies her. It pulls Meredith's body past the full-length mirror. She is blood-soaked and hungry, face crusted with bits of flesh and filth. The sight nearly makes her scream, but she can't let Meredith know what has happened.

Meredith reaches the back room and fights for control of herself. She tucks herself away in the black shadows behind the mound of things, and spies on her daughter from there. It's too dark in the house to see anything.

The living room light turns on and Allison screams.

Meredith can't see the living room from her position—it is obstructed by empty packages. But in clear view is Allison's face, stricken with terror as she stands over what must be the most gruesome sight she'd ever seen.

With all of her remaining strength and willpower, Meredith pushes on the back door. It flings open and the piles of boxes spill out of the house, along with Meredith.

Allison's screams pour out of the house with her, but Meredith has already gotten to her feet and charged into a full sprint toward the woods. Tree branches lash against her face. The Void tries to steer her back, but she is focused solely on getting it away from Allison.

Meredith doubles over with sharp pangs in her gut, but she pushes deeper into the woods.

It grows within, and around her, pulling her deeper inside of herself, but she runs. Sock-footed and cold, Meredith cuts through the darkness, bathrobe blowing behind her.

And the Void expands.

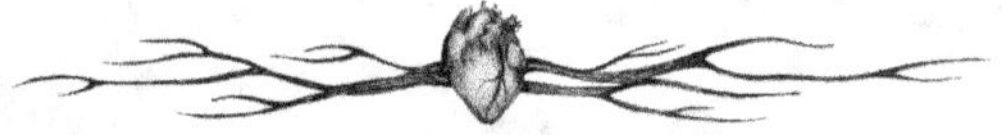

The Void that used to be Meredith crouches on the floor of an abandoned hunting shed, chewing on the tips of her own fingers. Surrounded by useless boxes of miscellany, she waits for another unsuspecting hunter to arrive. In the hours after it feeds, when Meredith is somewhat conscious, she tries to quell its hunger with things that used to satisfy. Packages—most of them pirated from neighborhood porches. But her attempts are futile, for these things are inadequate now. The Void requires more. Fingers gnawed to the bone, the raw flesh and open nerve endings sting, but the pain is a distant thing. More like the memory of a wound—an itchy scar. The taste of its own blood will appetize the Void until it can consume again.

Until then, it nibbles at the exposed bone on her forefinger.

Click. Click. Consume.

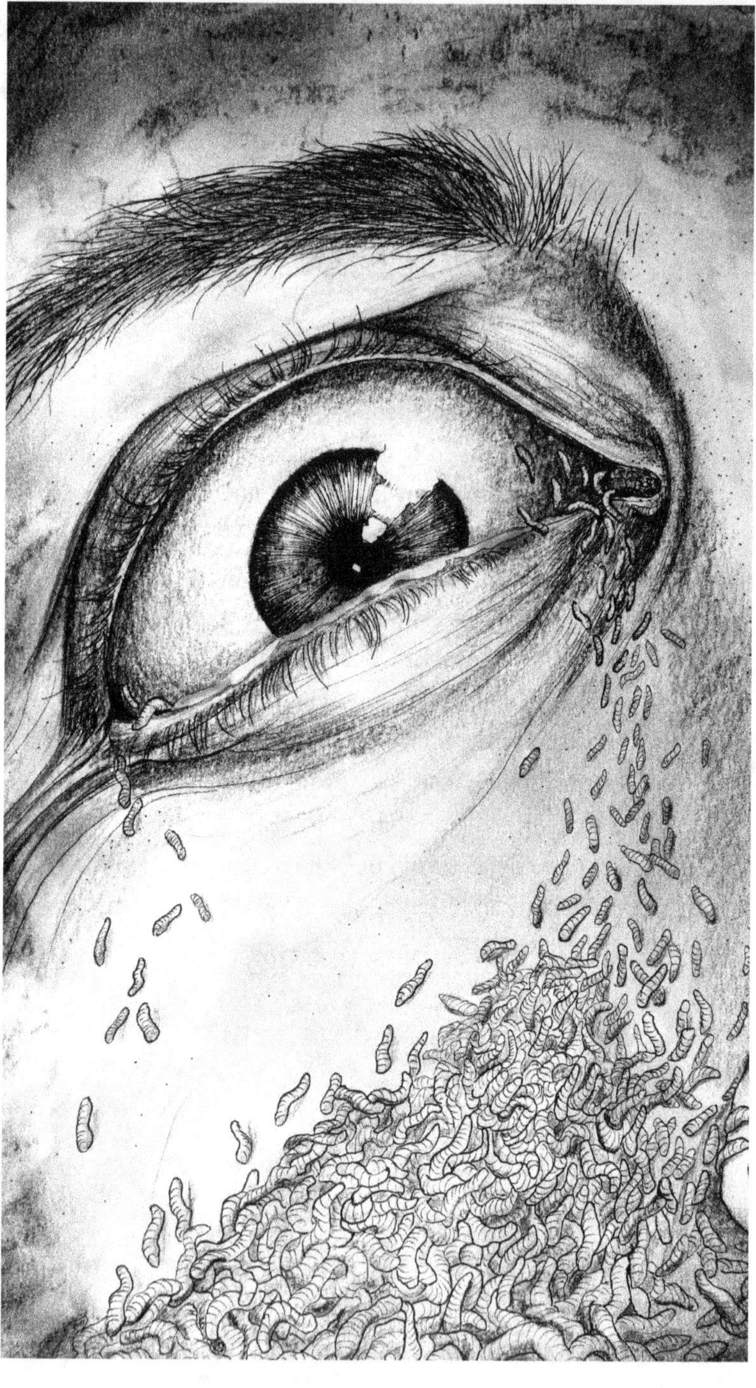

INFECTIOUS GLOW

Betelgeuse went supernova. There was never any guarantee that the massive red giant would blow within Chuck's lifetime. In fact, it was estimated that it could easily be a few hundred more years before it would happen. But then Chuck caught word through this astronomy club's social media group that it happened. Pushing 84 years old, and with a few too many close-calls on the old ticker, Chuck couldn't risk letting his heart give out before seeing it for himself. So he popped an aspirin and took some calming breaths to quell the excitement.

The other side of the planet witnessed it hours ago, and soon, Earth would rotate him to face the part of space where it had happened. Breaking news stories and images shared online across the amateur astronomy community, showed a bright light in the evening sky, arguably brighter than the moon. It washed out the glow of the stars all around it. Folks in Russia and Europe had been treated to what appeared to be a nebulous bulge against the backdrop of the night. The gaseous cloud which formed from the violent death of the star was described as being in brilliant reds and purples. Just Chuck's luck. As a colorblind individual, he'd never been able to distinguish reddish hues—not even the supposed ruddy color of the supergiant before it went supernova. Not even the rusty surface of Mars or those lovely carbon stars everyone likes to observe. For Chuck, he saw only a faint gray-white light, or occasionally a hint of brown if he was lucky.

Despite his lifelong inability to see those reds, Chuck took a liking to astronomy as a hobby from a young age. He'd dumped thousands—more like tens of thousands—on equipment over the years to catch photons from millions of years ago. Glimpses into the past. Little gray fuzzy blobs of light reaching him from eons ago, whispering that all is right in the universe, even when all on earth goes to shit.

This evening, as the city rotated out of the sun's light, and into the darkness of space, the constellation of Orion would be rising in the east, along with what was left of its star Betelgeuse.

He wished Marian could be here with him to view it. Not that she cared much for bundling up in winter coats to peek through an eyepiece at the little fuzzy blobs Chuck loved so dearly. But for this, she would have been right by his side.

His gear was packed into the cart, including his twelve-inch Dobsonian and the Takahashi for imaging. Binoculars. A reclining lawn chair. Chuck wheeled his cart into the hallway of the apartment complex. He was on the fourth floor—closest to the roof. It wasn't exactly dark skies up there, but the elevator made it convenient, and the landlord gave him a key to the rooftop lights so he could shut them off as he pleased. After Marian passed, he'd considered moving away from the city to darker skies, but he couldn't bring himself to leave.

His neighbor Devon approached from down the hall with his head down. Oversized headphones sat on top of a slouched knit hat. Skinny jeans so tight, Chuck was surprised he could walk in them. The kid's backpack was slung over a shoulder while a free hand thumbed at his phone.

Devon raised his eyes as he approached Chuck. "Got a big night planned?" His slow, stoner-like voice irritated Chuck.

"Ha! Are you kidding?"

Devon stared, mouth hanging open, and shrugged.

"Betelgeuse blew!"

"No way!" Devon staggered back a step.

"How have you not heard this? Don't you get news on that thing?" Chuck nodded to the kid's phone.

"I've been working all night." Devon's bloodshot eyes spoke of his exhaustion…or perhaps being stoned out of his gourd.

"Come up for the show as soon as it's dark. I'll let you look through the scope."

"Most definitely." Devon nodded. "Got some homework to do, and then I'm there."

Devon pulled his headphones back over his ears and continued down the hall. The college-aged kid wasn't the only oblivious one. It'd been a universal fact that most people had no idea what was going on right over their heads, every moment of every day. Billions of galaxies swirled and burned and collided. Stars collapsed and exploded. Remnant clouds of gas expanded and contracted… and the people just kept walking, eyes on the ground, eyes on their devices, never caring to look up until the news told them to. And the news was almost always wrong about when to look up.

But now, the headlines were everywhere.

Red Giant Goes Supernova!
Massive Stellar Explosion Visible from Earth!
Alien Life Sends Signal Across the Stars!
The End is Near!

Some of the headlines were ridiculous, and Chuck laughed them off. For every astronomical event, there was always some yahoo thinking the world was ending.

The elevator dinged, and Chuck rolled his cart into what he called the roof foyer. He opened the door to the outside world, and claimed a spot with the view of the southeast sky. Beyond the two-story building next door, Chuck had a view of the campus quad, and the west hill where the sun had recently set. Beyond that hill, out of view, was the cemetery where his dear Marian was buried.

"It's going to be quite the night, Marian."

Behind the atmosphere's twilight, the archer Orion was on his side, sparkling against a black backdrop. Soon, his shoulder, formed by the star Betelguese, would rise above the horizon with the rest of his stars.

An hour passed and the sky darkened. The faint glow of a cloud-like structure ascended. Another half hour passed and the bright glow shone into clarity. It was larger than the moon, which was below the horizon this evening. The most beautiful naked-eye object he'd ever seen. The nebula shifted gently against the darkening sky like the aurora borealis. He'd never seen anything like it.

"What the hell?" Chuck laughed with delight, or maybe insanity. It shouldn't have looked this way. Other astronomers had to be saying something about it online. They should've been spewing their crazy theories about why the nebula was moving like this, but there were no new notifications from his astronomy group.

On the street below and on rooftops across the way, people left the comfort of their homes to look at the magnificent sight. Clad in robes and flannels for a brief glimpse at the supernova, they stared with rapt and silenced awe. Chuck had never seen a non-astronomer so fascinated by the sky. Sometimes the public would be wowed by the craters of our moon, the rings of Saturn, or Jupiter's moons. Occasionally folks who truly appreciated the heavens would be dazzled even by the dull, little fuzzy blobs that were entire galaxies. But tonight, everyone was captivated by the universe's beauty.

Chuck's Takahoshi was set to automatically take photographs. With the strange shifting light, there'd be a good chance he'd get nothing but streaks and blurs. He gazed through his Dobsonian, but the central star where Betelgeuse had collapsed was far too bright to view. A wide field-of-view eyepiece would allow him a better look. He traced the nebulous dust as it shifted through the sky. There was something strangely magical about it.

Something living and breathing about the way it streamed and swirled upon the air… And then it occurred to him; this wasn't light from hundreds of lightyears away. It was atmospheric.

Impossible.

Another half-hour passed. He always lost track of time at the eyepiece, while the rest of the world around him fell away and he was part of the universe.

A few neighbors from downstairs opened the rooftop door, drawing Chuck's attention back to earth. Mrs. Gent with her two kids approached.

"We saw the news and thought you'd be up here," she said.

They were no strangers to looking through Chuck's eyepiece whenever he set up for the evening. Mrs. Gent gave a friendly smile and a wave, then ushered her children closer. He gestured for them to take a look while he fumbled with his phone, calling his astro-buddy, Mike. Chuck rubbed his itchy eyes and waited as the phone rang.

No answer.

Nothing posted in his group yet, either.

"I'm not sure what the heck that glow in the sky is, but it can't be from Betelgeuse." He looked up from the phone. Mrs. Gent and her kids' eyes were locked on the sky. Curtains of glowing, moving light reached from 500 light years away, and somehow appeared to enter our breathable air, hypnotizing the family of three.

"Mrs. Gent?"

She stared intently, slack jaw, eyes unblinking. Arms dangling loose by her sides. Her children did the same.

On the rooftop next door, others stood without movement as well. Upright, facing the east, but everything about them looked asleep.

The glaringly bright Betelgeuse rose to 45 degrees over the horizon. The gray-whites and blues of the nebulous cloud expanded outward.

Chuck grabbed Mrs. Gent by the shoulders and tried to break her gaze. "Mrs. Gent?"

There was no response as he gently shook her. The woman's spine and knees were locked steady. Gabby and Trey were in the same state. Chuck knelt down, bum knee trembling before landing on solid ground. He tried to lock eyes with Gabby—the smallest—in kindergarten, if he remembered correctly. Her brother Trey's hand dangled beside hers. He stood a foot taller, but Chuck had no clue how old the boy was. He had Marian for remembering that stuff.

Dark eyes reflected the hypnotic dance of photons in the sky.

Chuck slowly turned his head back to the sight. Back to the mysterious light. Dry eyes irritated Chuck to the point of breaking out his moisturizing drops. Sirens in the distance sounded. He wasn't sure how long they'd been going.

On the streets, people stood on sidewalks, gazing upon the sky.

Nobody moved.

Chuck pulled up his news app for information and the headlines appeared immediately. Reports of people in a hypnotic state. Thousands, tens of thousands, had been affected. He clicked a video. A shaking anchorwoman sat before the camera. "We're trying to reach an expert—*anyone* about what may be happening. For now, whatever you do, do NOT look at the supernova. Stay inside."

Hours-old reports flooded his search feed. European nations locked down while their people stared to the skies. It was everywhere. Happening to everyone—everyone but Chuck.

Chuck unplugged his computer and camera, and gathered them under his arms. With a moment of hesitation, he left the cart, the refractor, and the Dobsonian behind. He backed into the safety of the roof foyer and pressed the button to the elevator. His heart pounded and his head scrambled for answers, but nothing made sense.

Back in his apartment, Chuck closed his blinds, squeezing one more peek between the slats. The numbers of people on the street must've doubled. They all stood deathly still, faces following the light in the sky. Their bodies turned as Betelgeuse and its strange nebula slowly trekked higher into southern sky. As the earth rotated, so they did as well, tracking the sight like a guided telescope. Most of the cloud stayed in a bubble around Beteguese's bright center, but some of it trailed behind, leaving a strange arc along the ecliptic path.

Chuck paced the apartment, scratching his head, shaking himself as if from a terrible dream. God, he prayed it to be so. Prayed to finally be asleep. He'd had a hard go of this thing called life. Losing Danny when he was so young nearly killed Chuck. Then Marian's battle with cancer. Her years and years of sickness. Moving to the city where she could be closer to the center. The years he spent giving up his love of the night sky so he could be by her side whenever she needed him. Then after her passing, insomnia. The endless nights where nothing but the stars brought him light. Maybe, *maybe*, he was finally asleep.

But this dreadful reality was no better.

Chuck lay down on his bed, blinds drawn shut. He squeezed his lids together until tears eked out of dry eyes, soaking his lashes. Ragged breaths shuddered his heart. An ache in his left arm forced him to sit up.

Calm, relaxing breaths.

He reached for his bedside bottle of aspirin and popped a couple in his mouth to ward off another attack.

"Not now," he whispered to his failing heart. "Not now." But he wasn't sure why not. Why not let his heart go so he could be with his family again?

Looking at the news would only exacerbate his condition. He needed rest. He needed relaxed nerves and a cool mind, and then he'd figure it out. His head hit the pillow. Marian's side of the bed had been empty for a while now, but he liked to imagine her laying there beside him.

Sleep evading him, he forced his eyes closed and repositioned himself at least a dozen times.

Upon opening his eyes, giving up on the attempt to sleep, the clock on the nightstand read 6:00AM. Turns out he'd slept after all, but it didn't feel like it. The nerves in his body trembled as he swung his legs over the side of the bed and edged toward the window. He spread the blinds with two fingers and peeked down to the lamp-lit streets. Dawn's light barely kissed the horizon in the east. Hundreds of people now stood outside on the sidewalks and on the roofs. Some in their street clothes, some in scrubs, suits, or robes. Everyone faced west, where Betelgeuse would be setting soon.

All of his gear was hopefully still on the roof, untouched, and safe from any accumulating dew. It was a ridiculous thought to have at this moment—to be worried about dew on his gear. But his gear was Chuck's only window to everything that was left worth living for.

Chuck turned on the television—a digital TV with rabbit ears—Marian and he could never find anything good on cable or satellite, so it was one of the old-fashioned things that followed them into modern days. None of the usual major network channels came through. He popped another aspirin for preventative measure, then searched his browser for information on Betelgeuse and strange human behavior. Conspiracy blogs and unsubstantiated news reports plagued the internet. It was as if the reporters who were left unaffected couldn't get answers as to what was going on. So, they made up answers. Speculation flooded the screen.

Then he found reports coming out of South America and Australia, where Betelgeuse was not visible this time of year. The unaffected southern hemisphere shared stories that had come out of Russia, India, China, and the U.S. Folks were in a "zombie-like trance" all evening, staring upon Betelgeuse. But upon sunrise, the people became unglued from their positions and began to wander.

Some stumbled aimlessly, but many were violent upon awakening.

A viral video out of Russia, shared through an Australian news source, showed a man walking barefoot down a desolate road. The camera person recording it had been standing on his porch, documenting the white-out conditions from the storm, and what appeared to be blistering cold weather. When the man with the camera approached the barefoot straggler on the road, the straggler turned to face him. Lurching shoulders and awkward knee jerks moved him forward as if he was learning to walk for the first time. The camera person backed up as the man drew closer, asking something in Russian that Chuck couldn't understand. The straggler closed in with startling speed and the camera jerked away, falling to the snow. White nothingness covered the screen, but the distinct sound of gasping and gurgling tortured Chuck's imagination.

The sun would be up any moment. If these reports of people waking in a violent state were true, he'd need to get his things.

Chuck donned a thick, fleece-lined flannel and poked his head into the hallway. He hurried to the elevator.

Mrs. Gent and her kids remained standing on the roof, now facing the opposite direction to the west. They must've followed the ecliptic path of Betelgeuse all evening. That eerie curtain of light trailed the entire southern sky, from east to west, like a colorless rainbow. It moved above and below sparse clouds. Whatever it was, it was here on earth. Chuck's eyes burned, and he rubbed away the sensation.

"Mrs. Gent," he said, voice shaking. "Gabby? Trey?"

No response. Their skin had turned a faint shade of blue. Fingertips whitening. The rooftop people across the way suffered in the same state. Frost-bitten and hypothermic.

Chuck hurried to his cart and began to disassemble equipment, but breaking down his gear would take too long. Who knew what would happen once the light from Betelgeuse set? He disconnected the Takahoshi from its mount and laid it in the protective foam—now damp from dew and plummeting temperatures. Then movement below caught his eye. He peeked over the side of the building to the people on the street. All of them, at once began to walk, fanning out in different directions. None of them bothered to say a word to another. Their movements were awkward. Several tripped and crashed to the ground, as if their limbs were dysfunctional after being frozen solid all night. From their vantage point, Betelgeuse must've been out of sight. They woke up after it set…and if the reports were true, they would turn violent.

Chuck backed away from his equipment. From the rooftop, Betelgeuse was still in view, kissing the top of the hill.

Mrs. Gent and her kids remained still, but not for long.

Chuck hurried for the elevator door. He left his precious equipment behind. The elevator doors opened quickly and Chuck entered, rapid-firing at the close-door button.

Before the doors shut, little Gabby woke from her

trance and her blank eyes met with Chuck as the bell dinged. Trey did the same, then their mother. They all held their gaze on Chuck with the same rapt attention that locked them on Betelgeuse. As the doors closed, Mrs. Gent pushed past the children, stumbling toward Chuck.

He thought to hold the door. Maybe they weren't a danger. Maybe they needed help. He could've taken them to the hospital. All these thoughts rushed out as quickly as they galloped in. The elevator doors shut.

The bell dinged and the doors parted. Chuck pushed through unforgiving knee pain and crept quietly back to his apartment. The moment he closed his door, a banging vibrated through the wood.

"Chuck!" a voice said.

The door rattled with pounding from the other side. "Chuck!"

Heart racing, Chuck grabbed the baseball bat he kept in the corner, and tore open the door.

Devon stepped back, wide-eyed. Phone clenched tight in one hand. "I heard the elevator. Thought it was you."

"What the hell is going on?" Chuck said.

"I fell asleep early last night. I didn't see." Devon aimed his phone's screen at Chuck. The headline from the Australian news source read *The World Stops*.

The elevator dinged. Both Chuck and Devon turned in the hallway as the doors opened. Two small figures stepped into view—Trey and Gabby. Their mom, Mrs. Gent, followed. Knees wobbling, arms stretched to brace herself on the wall. Gabby stumbled to the left and fell to the floor, quickly righting herself with a leap to her feet.

The family's eyes were all fixed upon Chuck and Devon. Mother and children retched like cats about to puke. Eyes wide and bloodshot, Gabby stepped forward again. Then Trey. And their mother.

Devon pressed into Chuck's apartment, both men keeping their eyes on the family coming toward them. Limbs chaotic and awkward, like a pack of wolf pups learning to run. Hunger in their eyes, Mrs. Gent and her children closed in.

"Mrs. Gent?" Devon's voice shook as he shoved all the way into Chuck's apartment, away from them. Chuck shut the door and their bodies slammed into the other side.

Chuck's trembling hand locked the deadbolt. A hammering heart warned him to breathe easily. It thump-thumped and sputtered, chugging to keep up with his mind and body.

Banging, thrashing, and scratching at the door. Sweat dripped from Chucks' sparse white hair and dribbled into his eye. Salty perspiration seeped into chapped lips. He kept his weight pressed against the door as they rammed it mindlessly.

"What's wrong with them?" Devon helped to brace the door with his arms, leaning into it.

Every bang against the wood sent an interruption into Chuck's steadying heart.

"Everything okay out here?" A voice called from farther down the hall.

Devon's eyes widened as the banging ceased.

"Ma'am? You okay?" The man's voice drew closer.

Mrs. Gent and her children were silent. Footsteps

shuffled away from the door, drawing their shadows from under the gap.

Chuck rolled over and fought his knees to get up.

Devon twisted the deadbolt, which clicked like a shotgun blast no matter how slow it turned. His eyes met with Chuck's briefly before twisting the knob. The door opened only a crack and they squeezed their faces close to get a peek into the hall.

"Hey!" a man at the end of the hall said to Mrs. Gent. The family's backs were to Chuck now. "You need help?"

The man wore a robe—Chuck forgot his name. It was Brian or Bryce or Braxton or something. Instead of veering back into his apartment, the man drew closer to Mrs. Gent and the kids.

Devon stepped into the hall. He stood like a man ready to run…or maybe one ready to fight. His feet were planted solid, one foot in front of the other, elbows bent, prepared for whatever was to come. Chuck wasn't sure if the kid was going to try to dash after them and play hero, or if he was ready to throw punches if they turned around and came back.

It was absurd that Mrs. Gent and these kids seemed like such a threat. They were harmless. Innocents. Not a bad bone in their bodies. Chuck had high hopes for little Gabby, who was the most impressed person to ever look through his telescope. She could name all of the Galilean moons. That was unheard of for a girl her age. Hell, most adults couldn't even identify Jupiter.

His mind raced through so many thoughts as the awkward clumsy family crashed into Braxton-Brian-

Bryce at the end of the hall.

The man's eyes latched onto Chuck as he fell to the floor with a grunt. Gabby crawled over him as he flailed. From Chuck's angle, it was hard to see, but she hovered her face over his.

Gabby's mouth opened wide and she retched. A pink substance spilled forth. A vomit akin to rice and raw meat spewed from the little girl onto the man's face. He screamed, thrashed, and threw Gabby into the wall before scrambling onto his knees.

A screech from the stairwell beyond drew Mrs. Gent's attention away.

Chuck's pulse pounded between his ears as he stood petrified, watching. All he could do was *watch*. His muscles, his will to run to the man's aid, it all froze solid—as stiff as the people who couldn't stop staring at the supernova. Mrs. Gent and Trey stepped over the squirming man on the floor and headed to the stairwell after the screams.

Gabby climbed to her feet. She gazed down the hall for a moment as Brian—Chuck decided his name was Brian—writhed on the floor.

Chuck and Devon backed into the apartment before being seen. Another piercing shriek from outside. Sirens blared in the distance.

Gabby stumbled forward, hit the button on the elevator doors and stepped inside.

At the end of the hall, Brian sat upright. His head twitched from side to side. Arms fell limp to the floor. His spine was slumped, like a ragdoll coming to life.

Spying from the cracked door, Devon whispered. "We should check on him."

But before taking action, the pink vomitous substance that Gabby had spewed all over the floor and onto Brian's face, had begun to move. The squirming larva-like mass climbed Brian's body, disappearing beneath fabric and into his hairline. It squiggled down his face and entered eye sockets, ears.

Chuck's stomach lurched and he quickly covered his mouth to hold back the contents of his stomach. He choked it down, then snatched a wad of Devon's shirt between his shoulder blades to keep him from going into the hall. The same grab he made for his boy Danny when he was a toddler. About to run into traffic, or plow through someone at the mall, Chuck would snatch Danny's shirt to keep him from utter catastrophe.

"Wait," Chuck said, with his fingers clenched tight to the boy's fabric. "Something ain't right."

Brian climbed to his feet. His body undulated, wormlike for—Chuck counted—six, seven, eight seconds. Brian stood lifeless, any sign of humanity scrubbed clean from his face. The stairwell door flung open and a woman ran screaming from inside.

"Help me!" Outstretched arms reached for Brian.

Stomping feet on the stairwell followed her.

Brian opened his arms, grabbed the woman in a bear hug and pulled her to the floor. Pink excretions poured like a deluge from his mouth, over her face.

And then more blank-faced people entered the hall.

Chuck yanked Devon back and closed the door,

securing the locks.

His fingers were still clenched tight to the fabric of Devon's shirt. Knuckles ached as he loosened his grip.

Devon paced. "What the fuck?" His voice shook. "What…" He gestured toward the door. "…the. fuck." Devon sat on the recliner, elbows propped on his knees, head in his hands, squeezing tufts of black curly hair between his fingers.

Chuck opened his laptop. There needed to be more information out there, somewhere. He scoured the search engines for news again. Australian, Brazilian, and South African news sources remained online. Speculation was all they had to go on. And all they knew was that everyone who gazed upon the supernova was affected.

"Did you see it last night?" Chuck asked.

Devon rocked in his seat, clinging to his phone like a lifeline, scrolling.

"Hey kid!"

Devon snapped to attention. "No! I think that's why I'm okay. They're saying if you looked…but *you* looked." Devon stood, right foot slid in front of the other, prepared again to either run or fight.

Chuck nodded. "But nothing happened to me."
"Why?"

Chuck went back to the screen for answers—or at least ideas that could lead to some kind of reasonable explanation. His eyes itched. "I don't know."

"It can't be the supernova," Devon said. "If you were looking at it…"

"Then what?"

"Parasitic," Devon said. "Those things that Gabby threw up all over that guy's face. It got into him. I don't know any parasite that works that fast though." Devon's demeanor changed. He paced, but less frantically. He paced as if he were contemplating. Furrowed brow. Hands tightened into fists, biting his lip. He went to the window and paused.

"But they all—every one of them—the reports said that the moment they saw the light in the sky, they froze. They were in some kind of trance," Devon said.

"It's true," Chuck said. "I saw it myself last night with the Gents. As soon as the glow of Betelgeuse was above the horizon, everyone stopped and didn't move again until the light set this morning."

"Light... Information…parasites and light?" Devon whispered random words.

Chuck feared the poor stoner kid was losing it.

"And what's this cloud in the sky?" he said. "The streaky blue and red glow—like northern lights."

"Don't look at it!" Chuck hurried to his side.

Devon turned around quickly. "Shit…" closed his eyes like he was awaiting an inevitable death, but nothing happened. "I feel fine."

Chuck looked out the window at the faint cloud of swirling dust.

"What is that?" Devon asked.

"It's in our atmosphere. I saw it move in front of a cloud. But, somehow it trails Betelguese's path along the ecliptic." Chuck made an arc with his hand from east to west.

"It's dissipating." Devon leaned closer to the window.

"Or daylight is washing out its glow… no. I think you're right. The cloudiness of it does seem more sparse now. I see some faint blue hues—but the gray in-between spaces don't seem as bright. That's the red, right? Is there any more red?"

Devon's face showed his confusion.

"Colorblind." Chuck squinted out the window.

Devon shook his head. "No. I don't see any red at all. What if that cloud is carrying the parasites?"

"Aerosolized parasites? Like a bio-weapon?"

"I don't know…" Devon chewed his bottom lip, then felt the frame of the window. "These windows are solid right? Not too drafty?"

Chuck stepped away from the window. The thought of an aerosolized parasite squeezing between the cracks, into the vents, and into his bodily orifices made him shudder. Those rice squigglies wriggling into his mouth, taking over his body until he was nothing but a shell of a human… Chuck's neck tensed and he focused on a deep breath to relax the muscles.

Devon jumped. "A hoax—a diversion. A bio-weapon let loose across the world. But to get more people exposed, they staged a fake supernova explosion. Made it look like Betelgeuse blew so that more people would be infected as they looked up to the sky."

Chuck shook his head. "Betelgeuse definitely went supernova. Amateur astronomers all over the world were looking through backyard telescopes, taking astro-images and uploading in real time. I must've seen hundreds of images of auto-uploaded raw images before they went silent. I saw it myself. You can't hoax something like that."

Devon growled. "Supernova. Light. Information. Parasites... Some bacterium are photosensitive. They need light."

Chuck raised an eyebrow, surprised by the stoner kid.

"I study microbiology. I just earned my bachelors in biology and I'm now going for a PhD. So it's kind of my thing."

Chuck was taken aback. "I just thought you were a dumb stoner."

"That's funny. I just thought you were a miserable old man."

Chuck huffed, and scrolled again. "It's all impossible. None of it adds up."

"But why not *you*?" Devon stared intently at Chuck. "Is it because you're colorblind."

"How does being colorblind have anything to do with infection?"

"It doesn't."

"My cones don't process red light."

"So what is it about the red light?" Devon's eyes darted back and forth. "Red light...Parasite." It was like watching an AI calculate information in some terrible sci-fi movie.

"Red light carrying information?" Chuck asked. He wasn't sure where the kid was going, it was all very far-fetched, but grasping at straws was all they had. "Maybe that's why I didn't get hypnotized. My eyes were bugging me last night. They were itchy. What if those things were sending information on the red light?" Chuck burst out laughing. "Nevermind. I sound like a quack!"

"And then there's Schroedinger's Bacterium."

Chuck waited for more. He'd heard of Schroedinger's Cat, but never this.

"Okay, hear me out." Devon paced, rubbing his hands. He chuckled a little "This is insane."

"So is everything we've experienced."

"There was a study done years ago—2018, 2019, I think. I remember reading the article. This study was done linking a connection of some bacterium and light and quantum physics. They suggested the possibility of quantum entanglement between photosynthetic organisms. *Organisms!* These green sulfur bacterium live in the deep ocean where there's, like, no light. But they photosynthesize somehow—and quantum biology is one of the theories. Being in two places at once. Where there is light, and where there isn't."

Chuck sighed. "This is all…"

"Theoretic, and completely bonkers. Yeah. I know." Devon held up a finger. "But what do we know? Betelgeuse went supernova. That's a fact, correct?"

"Yeah."

Devon's eyes were wild, wide and excited. "And it's a fact that when Betelgeuse went supernova, there was also an appearance of a cloud in our atmosphere—the glowy red and blue stuff, right?"

Chuck nodded.

"So, we don't know if this is causation or correlation,

but it's feeling really fucking causation-y, you know?"

Chuck interjected. "Even at the speed of light, it would take 500 years for anything to get here. This supernova happened that long ago. And nothing travels at light speed, other than light. And if some bacteria could travel at the speed of light, nothing survives 500 years in space."

"But hear me out. *If* there is microbial life out somewhere near Betelgeuse. Which isn't an outrageous thing to believe. And *if* that microbial life is dependent on—let's say—*red light* somehow to do a quantum entanglement thing—"

"Quantum entanglement thing?" Chuck's confidence in the kid's theory waned.

"Look, man. I'm not a physics major. I don't know a damn thing about the quantum realm. I'm just brain-vomiting here… What if this is some kind of bacterium—or in this case, some kind of parasite—that was threatened with the blow of its life-giving star, and in its last desperate attempt for survival, it quantum-jumped here?"

"Like that old TV show Quantum Leap?"

Devon rolled his eyes. "I don't know what that is. But there's a cloud of red light that hypnotized the world, hijacked some brains, and let in some potentially aerosolized parasites. And now everyone is infected. Except for the folks who didn't look. And except for the folks who didn't have the proper receptors to process that red light, initially…Still doesn't add up." Devon rubbed his forehead.

"Maybe they traveled here by some red light quantum

leap." Chuck laughed. "But they're here and spreading. We can see the wormy little bastards ourselves. Those aren't aerosolized. I bet if those little larva guys got inside me, I wouldn't stand a chance, colorblind or not."

Devon shook his head. "Probably not…" He let out a maniacal laugh. "That's so crazy! That can't even be what happened. It can't! That's… There has to be a less crazy idea." He looked to Chuck.

"Sorry kid, I've got nothing."

Screams in the street drew Chuck and Devon back to the window. A shriek gurgled into silence before they could spot what had happened. Scattered people shuffled down the street. Arms limp. Legs making chaotic, over-corrected steps.

"They're like fucking zombies, man," Devon said.

Chuck hated that the kid was right. They were like zombies. Every one of them. Mindless. Bodies driven by some other inhuman force. Some raging infection from those little pink squigglies eating away at their brains until they were nothing but walking carcasses, intent on spreading themselves among the human population.

For a moment, he was relieved that Marian left this world before this happened, but he also wished she were by his side to calm his nerves. She had a way about her. She'd press two fingers into that little divot at the back of his neck, just under his skull. She'd press that spot and hold, almost like she was slowing the rush of blood to his head, slowing his mind, slowing his pulse.

Devon checked his phone. "He's alive." His eyes gleamed with hope. "My friend at the university. I have to get to him."

Chuck shook his head. "Son, please. Don't think about going out there."

"The red glow—I can't see it anymore." He gestured out the window. "The aerosolized stuff is gone. I can risk it."

"But why?"

"It's the university. Food. Shelter. Strong doors."

"And thousands of people, probably throwing up that pink rice all over the campus."

"This all went down overnight. Only a handful of people are in the building overnight. Everyone else is on the other side of campus at the dorms. My friend is in the lab with a few others…maybe we can figure this out. We have one of the best labs in the country."

"What are you going to do? Gather up some of those worm things and go do tests on them?"

"I don't know. Maybe. *Someone* should."

"I think it's best if we wait it out here for a while. Let's see if the government is doing anything."

"The government doesn't give a shit about us!"

"I think it's smarter if we give it a couple days."

"I'm not leaving him alone for a couple days!" Tears reached the rim of his lower lids. Rage swirled in his desperate eyes. The kind of rage that bubbled up when a man was kept from the one he loved. Chuck felt the same anger fill his heart, his soul, all the way to his eyeballs, when he'd learned of his wife's terminal illness, after God had taken so much already. Angry with the doctors, angry with his wife for letting it go for so long, angry with God...

"He's a good friend?" Chuck asked.

"Yeah…" Devon stared out the window. "He's my boyfriend."

"Casual or serious?"

"What do you care?"

"Because if this is someone you barely know, it's not worth the risk. But if he means something to you, then that's a different story."

"He means something."

"Okay then." Chuck slid his arms into his fleece-lined flannel and began to button it up. "I'll go with you." What the hell did it matter? Chuck couldn't live out his last days starving to death in his apartment. In the depressing one bedroom where his wife succumbed to the cancer inside her. The place where his son never spent a moment of his life. Danny never got to see anything beyond the age of eight because of Hodgkins. What was left to do in this miserable world other than look at the stars, then die? There was nothing left for Chuck. But he could at least help this kid try to do something. Try to save the world, or whatever he thought he was going to do. Save his love. Be with the one he needed to be with. That's all people have—their loves. Of life, of each other, of art and nature…

"You don't have to do that, Chuck."

"You said it yourself. The university has food and a lab. And, no doubt one of those departments has a communications system, and of course, backup generators. It's a smart call."

"Maybe we should wait until dark? Sneak through the

shadows, you know?"

"When it's dark, Betelgeuse will be rising again. What if it throws off some of that light stuff again? What if gets in you?"

"What if I go out now and it gets in my eyes?" Devon says.

"You could close your eyes…"

"And what? Bird Box my way to the lab in a blindfold?"

"What's a bird box?"

"It's a movie."

Chuck looked out the window to the building across the street. Below, fewer and fewer people could be spotted walking. "Where are they going?"

"Probably to find more hosts? The zombie-ant fungus gets into an ant and hijacks its body so it can reproduce. The ant walks around under control of the fungus."

"They're finding more people? *What* people?" Half the damn planet has laid their eyes on the supernova by now. The major network news stations aren't reporting. What happens when everyone is gone?"

The vantage point from the roof gave a view of the streets with straggling souls wandering below. The chill of the crisp air bit his nose. The crowds thinned. Beyond the next building, the campus quad had few people, unlike the hundreds from earlier. Chuck's breaths amplified in his gas mask. Devon wore Marian's old mask from the 2020 pandemic. The masks were equipped with goggles and ventilators. Chuck had saved them all these years just in case.

"Do you think they're in the buildings?" Chuck asked.

"Ryan says the main building is secure."

"Where the hell did they all go?"

Devon shook his head. "If they're looking for more people, maybe they're leaving town. Maybe they've gotten everyone here and they're moving on...other mammals? Crossing the equator and spreading into the southern hemi? It's all a guess. Until we know more about this thing, everything is a wild guess. One of the guys with Ryan lives on the coast. It's not that far. He's got a boat...like, a yacht, I guess. They're talking about sailing south."

Chuck nodded and tried to comfort himself. "I've never seen the southern hemisphere's sky. That might be nice."

The path straight to the school would leave them wide open. Driving would only attract attention. Devon assured Chuck they could slip through the park down the street under the cover of high hedges until they reached the fringe of campus. From there, they'd climb the west hill and follow the ridge, down the other side to the lab.

Devon's backpack was strapped on, packed full of supplies which Chuck helped him curate for the short but dangerous trek across campus and beyond. A lighter, flashlight, utility knife, dry clothes and socks, typical backwoods camping gear. He held a baseball bat in one hand in case he needed to protect himself. It reminded Chuck of sending Danny off on his first day of kindergarten. Shoving him out into the cruel world to survive.

"Ryan's expecting us. They have the main entrance doors barricaded, but the back entrance to the lab will be easy to get to. They'll be there to let us in."

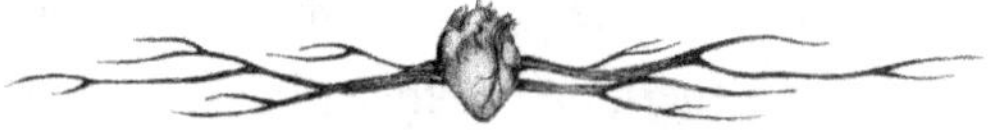

Chuck and Devon hurried along the sidewalk, close to the buildings, tucked in long shadows as the evening sun fell behind the buildings. Betelgeuse would rise again soon. Overhead, song birds soared, flitting around as if nothing had happened, unaffected by the crumbling world.

They turned into the small park, staying low, concealed behind hedges. Behind them, a click drew their attention. They crouched to a pause as a straggler stumbled into a vehicle. The woman studied the door, head unstable on her shoulders. She grabbed at the car door handle and pulled.

"What the—" Devon whispered.

The straggly woman flung open the door, nearly falling over. She corrected herself and dove headfirst into the vehicle's driver side. After sitting right, she put her hands on the wheel. No key. No ignition. No attempt to shift. She rocked forward and back, in some mindless attempt to drive. Some small motor memory of how things worked allowed her to open the door and try to drive somewhere. Just like earlier with Gabby, opening the elevator doors.

Chuck's masked breaths echoed in his head. His speeding heart joined the song. Devon raced forward, young legs carrying him with ease. He looked back frequently, and slowed his pace to allow Chuck to keep up.

Good kid.

The hill was torture on Chuck's knees. He weaved to remain in shadows, tucked close to the shrubbery as they climbed. Nearing the crest of the hill—the ridge which divided the campus from the cemetery—a grunt came from below.

Devon dropped to the ground on his belly, propped up on elbows, he crawled to the edge of a bush. Below, dozens of the infected amassed. The graveyard like the bottom of a bowl too difficult for the infected to escape. Fenced on all sides, with the exception of the ridge which acted as a natural barrier. Sinking sunlight skimmed the gravestones and heads of the wandering masses.

Chuck gasped at the thought of any of them desecrating his wife's grave with their vile excretions. His neck tightened. A sharp pain in his shoulder followed, forcing an unexpected yelp from his lips. He grabbed his left arm. The ache was so intense he couldn't get up.

Focus on breathing.

He dug into his shirt pocket and popped an aspirin, swallowing it dry.

Devon didn't tell him to hurry. He didn't ask what was wrong. The boy knew. He looked Chuck in the eyes and figured it out. Smart kid.

He'll be all right.

One of the stragglers below must've heard Chuck's yelp and he began its ascent up the west slope.

The ache traveled down Chuck's arm and spread across his chest.

Breathe.

Devon hurried to his side and flung Chuck's arm over his shoulder.

"You better get going," Chuck said.

"Shut up and move."

But the pain paralyzed him. If he kept moving, his heart would give out. Chuck slumped to the ground. The sun slipped below the horizon, shifting the contrasting black shadows and sunlight into a steady even shade of gray.

The straggler closed in quickly. Chuck held out an arm to hold him off while Devon drove in with a blow to his head. The bastard's neck twisted and snapped. A spray of pink dusted the air and the straggler fell, rolling back down the hill.

Devon dropped to Chuck's side. "Can you walk?"

Down the hill, none of the others seemed to be alerted to their presence.

The aspirin worked at thinning Chuck's blood—at helping his heart to keep beating for now. Chuck wiped a bead of sweat from his brow. When he lowered his hand, a pink thing wriggled on his thumb. Before he could swat it away, it burrowed beneath his fingernail.

Chuck flailed, then squeezed his thumb to keep it from going further. Beneath the skin, he felt it squirm. It dug deep, slipping into his veins.

"We'll dig it out," Devon said, breaths becoming more frantic.

"There's not enough time for that." A sensation itched under his skin, squirming through his veins up his arm.

"Come on!" Devon said.

"You should get going."

"I'm not leaving you here."

"And I'm not going into that building with this thing inside of me," Chuck raised his voice.

Through Devon's gas mask, there was a hitch in his voice. "Jesus, Chuck."

A wave of numbness swept over his left arm. Inside, he knew the creature was multiplying, spreading, taking over his body. His nerves sparked in protest and Chuck let out another outburst.

This time, several people down the hill had heard his outcry. Their attention turned toward them, and they began their ascent.

"Time to go, Devon." Chuck removed his mask and handed it over.

Devon accepted it with reluctance in his eyes.

"Go save someone that can be saved." Chuck slid his pack from his back and tossed it to Devon's feet.

Devon looked to the sky, defeated, then back to Chuck before taking off with the supplies. It was a short trip to the side door, where a group of brilliant young people just like Devon would be waiting to let him in. Devon disappeared beyond the crest of the hill.

Chuck lay on his back in the cold grass as one man came into view, working his way to the crest. Overhead, the sky darkened to a deep blue. The orange horizon melted into purple.

The echo of a loud door slammed shut, and Chuck knew Devon was now safely inside the university.

A star shone above, piercing the twilight sky. Capella. To the east, the brilliant exploded Betelgeuse rose again.

The infected man stumbled over the top of Chuck.

His heart pounded with anticipation, but the man continued his course, uninterested in Chuck, whose body had already been taken.

Chuck let out a sigh and stared back to the sky. To his love. To the only reason worth living anymore. A wave of nausea coursed through his body, but his heart slowed. His heart calmed. At the back of his neck, that little divot at the base of his skull, he felt pressure. The gentle touch of loving hands. Marian's two fingers pressed against him, calming his heart and his mind. Existing here with him in this moment, while simultaneously decomposing at the bottom of the hill. He took one deep breath, knowing that they'd exist together always, no matter where they were. Chuck exhaled one last time—one final escape into the universe.

ARACHNU

Jamiah hated autumn. He hated the cold. He hated rotting pumpkins and dead leaves. He hated pumpkin spice lattes and pumpkin spice bread… soon, he was certain, there'd be pumpkin spice deodorant and pumpkin spice condoms. More than anything, he hated that in the fall, all the creepy crawlies tried to move indoors. Especially the spiders. They spend all summer outside where they belong, weaving clumps of webs in the grass. Or they'd claim the shady boughs in the pines lining his property. But in the fall, when the temps began to drop, more and more spiders would make an appearance in his house.

As a six-foot-two man with broad shoulders, nobody would ever suspect he'd need his wife to capture and release the spiders for him. If he had his way, he'd kill every last one that entered his home.

"They're not welcome in my house! It's breaking and entering," he'd told Alyssa.

"I'm pretty sure the spiders are just *entering*, you big

baby. There's no breaking."

"They're breaking my rules. No spiders."

"He's not hurting anyone."

"Just kill it."

"It didn't do anything wrong…" She scooped a spider the size of her thumbnail into a cup. "You want them dead, go ahead and step on it yourself next time."

Jamiah couldn't even do that. The feel of its body bursting under the sole of his shoe may as well have been the spider's hairy legs digging into his bare foot. The sensation was unbearable.

Alyssa stayed home in Pennsylvania, while Jamiah moved into the Virginia Beach property he'd closed on last week. The windows were wide open, allowing ventilation and a gentle autumn breeze through the house. Late October wasn't nearly as cold here as in Pennsylvania. He could get used to this temperate climate.

Jamiah used the back of his pry bar to yank up another square of asbestos-coated 1960's floor tile. Masked and gloved, he threw chunks of tile into a bucket and moved on to the next section, making his way across the 1000 square foot home which would soon become a money-making rental property.

He bought it as-is and sight-unseen, after the house foreclosed. He knew it was a financial risk, but a few grand and a little spit-shine would have the place paying for itself in no time. The winters were relatively mild this far south, so he and Alyssa could at least escape the unforgiving cold of Pennsylvania each year, and have a little beach house to enjoy.

As he yanked the last row of tiles from the hallway, he exposed a crack in the cement slab foundation.

"What the hell is this?" He ran his finger along the crack, which was almost wide enough to squeeze a pinky into. Movement within the crevice made Jamiah jump to his feet. A spider squeezed out of the foundation. It faced him, as if calculating his every move. Jamiah pressed his back as tight as he could against the wall as the spider adjusted its stance to watch him.

Arachnophobia—he knew every bit of his fear was irrational, but it didn't matter. It was palpable and real. The fear was like cement in his veins. He would have stomped the spider, but he couldn't muster the strength to lift his leg. He remained plastered to the wall, certain that if he took a single step, the spider would match his movement and lunge at his face.

A knock on the door was the catalyst he needed to hurry out of the hallway, away from the eight-legged menace. The plumber stood outside the storm door wearing blue coveralls; the company nametag on his chest read "Barry."

"Hey, man. Come on in." His nerves stopped firing as if they were in critical danger, and Jamiah relaxed his shoulders, glancing down the hall to see if the spider was still there. It had relocated out of sight. Maybe back in the crack, or into the hallway utility closet. Perhaps it scurried into the bathroom to hide under the toilet, ready to surprise Jamiah later while he took a dump.

"The toilet was backed up," Jamiah told the plumber. "Sewage overflowed up through the tub drain."

"Mhmm…" Barry scratched his greasy head.

"I snaked the drain and it cleared. It's flushing now just fine, but the drain snake pulled back some clay."

Barry shook his head. "Sounds like you got a busted pipe."

"Figured that much."

"These houses in this neighborhood all had to have the original plumbing replaced within the last ten years or so. That's probably what you need."

"What's that gonna cost me?"

"I'll work up an estimate."

Barry went to work running a camera through the drain, confirming the busted pipe somewhere under the washer-dryer hookup.

"Did you notice that the slab dips here?" he asked.

"What do you mean?"

Barry showed him how the floor seemed to slope at the center of the house. A slight gradual slant with the foundation crack right along the center. "Y'all's pipes might be the least of your problems. You should call someone about a foundation repair. Bet the ground is eroding away under your house."

"What the hell can cause that?"

"My guess… your cracked pipe is leaking into the ground under your house. Probably shifting the earth and creating a bit of a sinkhole."

"Son of a bitch!"

Alyssa was going to be pissed. She'd suggested a house in Florida for a vacation rental. She had one picked out and it was a toss-up between the two properties, but

Jamiah had to have the cheaper option. He took a risk and it bit him in the ass. He'd have to figure something out to make this pay off, or Alyssa would be using this "I told you so" for the rest of their lives.

Plumbing problems. Now a foundation repair. Add those to the smaller issues like poor insulation and a gas stove that wouldn't light without putting a lighter to the burner.

Another spider crept along the edge of the threshold as Jamiah walked Barry to the front door. Jamiah jumped, but tried to contain his fear.

Barry noticed and chuckled. "Just a wolf spider."

"Guess I gotta add pests to my list of problems. Know any good exterminators?"

"Yeah, I know one." Barry stomped on the wolf spider and grinned. "It's called Boot Pest Control!" He chuckled, then handed Jamiah the estimate.

When Jamiah's eyes peeled away from the arachnid carcass on his threshold, he looked at the bottom number on the estimate. "Are you serious? Twelve grand? Just for the plumbing?"

Barry cringed. "I know. But these slab homes require us to dig up the concrete just to access the pipes underneath. And there's damage all along the pipe, so we have to dig a trench through your house to get to it…" He scratched his oily hair again.

Jamiah sighed. "How much to just burn the house down?"

After Barry left belly-laughing over Jamiah's arson joke, the spiders kept creeping in.

He picked up four different kinds of bug sprays. Aerosol cans for instant-kill action and perimeter sprays to keep the bugs out. He walked the outside of the house, spraying the base of the cement slab and around every window. While spraying, wolf spiders dropped from under the yellow siding. He nearly died each time it happened. His heart wasn't built for this kind of stress. Good thing Alyssa started feeding him healthy over the last year—black bean burgers and more salad any man could ever imagine—or he probably would've had a coronary three spiders ago. He held his hand to his heart, giving himself a moment to recover from the trauma. Certain he sprayed them, he could assume they'd be dead in the overgrown grass within minutes.

As he rounded the last corner of the house back to the front yard, a blonde woman from next door waved and smiled.

"Hi!" She took a long drag off the butt of a cigarette, then threw it to the ground, stomping it out. She stuffed her hands in her back pockets—or maybe she was grabbing her own ass, Jamiah couldn't tell from his vantage point—and she walked toward him, meeting him halfway between their houses.

Jamiah waved as she approached.

"I'm Dana. Are you my new neighbor?"

He thought about telling her it was going to be a rental, but unsure how'd she'd take it, he simply said, "That's me."

"Welcome! It's nice to see someone will be living here again. It's been months!"

"I'm just working on fixing it up now."

"Did they leave it a mess in there?"

"It's empty…just old and needs a lot of work." Jamiah was about to excuse himself—segway into getting back to all that work that needed to be done, but she kept talking.

"The last people who lived there were really weird."

Oh no…a gossiper. His opportunity to escape the conversation was shrinking.

"They had people coming and going all the time. Dan—my husband—says they were into some kind of cult over there."

"A cult?"

"They had meetings all the time. It was always quiet though. Ella down the street said she heard chanting in there one night when she walked her dog by." Dana crossed her arms over her body. "Just, weird."

"Well—"

"And then, poof! Gone." She interrupted. "Up and left. No sign of them… Good riddance, am I right?"

"I guess," Jamiah said, surprised he was able to get two more words into the conversation. "I should really get back to work. Running out of daylight hours." he thumbed over his shoulder toward his house.

"You know…" She leaned in. "I wonder if it wasn't a cult, but some sort of weird sex thing." Her eyebrows arched.

Jamiah cringed and backed toward the front door.

"I'm just kidding!" she said, matching his steps,

following him. "Anyway, I'm glad you're moving in… as long as you're not part of some sex cult." She winked and elbowed his arm.

"Nope… can't say that I am." He'd rather deal with one of the spiders now, than her. He kept edging away.

She stopped, bit her lip, and made strong eye contact. "Too bad."

He lifted his left hand and twisted his wedding band, hoping she would get the hint. "Okay! I'm gonna get back—"

"Oh, I'm just playing." She waved airily. "I like to have fun and make jokes…"

He grabbed the handle of his front door, but she wasn't leaving.

"Do you drink?" she asked.

"My *wife* and I have an occasional Friday martini."

"Perfect! I have a housewarming gift for you."

"You do?"

"I got this bottle of vodka—it's very strong. I'm more of a chardonnay girl. Anyway, I'll bring it by later. Our other neighbor makes the best coffee, too. I'm sure she'll be stopping by with her famous latte."

"That's not necessary, but I appreciate the thought." He cracked open the door. "I gotta get back to it now. Nice to meet you, Dana."

"It was nice to meet you!"

He locked the front door behind himself. After cleaning up busted floor tiles, he set up for his first night in the house. His blow-up mattress in the corner offered no comfort because all he could imagine were the wolf spiders creeping up along the wall beside his bed. So, he pulled the mattress into the middle of the bedroom and sat on his island, watching the floor for more invaders, but none came. He'd talked to his wife on the phone, avoiding the part about the foundation and plumbing. He'd tell her eventually, but he wanted to feel like he had matters under control before making her worry about money.

He lay on the mattress, tossing and turning, trying to find the best way to get comfortable, when he spotted a shadow on the closet molding. The leggy, dark spot remained fixed until Jamiah sat up. Then it shifted toward the open closet.

Jamiah crept out of the bedroom for something to smack it with, and was going for his shoe until he saw the pry bar was much closer. He grabbed the iron bar in his palm, then moved into the bedroom and flicked the switch. The spider darted around the corner on the inside edge of the closet frame. Jamiah chased after, pry bar raised, both hands gripping it firmly. There's no way he'd sleep knowing it was in the room.

As he neared the closet, the spider's body squeezed behind the molding into a gap between the wall and the trim.

"Aw, hell no. You ain't getting off that easy." Jamiah tapped the frame with his pry bar and jumped back, expecting it to rush out. Nothing happened. He gave it another smack. Hitting the molding up and down, each blow getting harder. The wooden trim cracked and then peeled away from the wall completely, pulling a slab of drywall back in one piece.

"Shit!" He jumped away, thinking the whole wall was coming down, but it stayed upright. It simply opened, like a hidden passage beside the closet.

The two-foot wide door remained ajar while Jamiah leaned to get a look in the closet. There was dead space behind the secret door that wasn't part of the closet or the hallway.

Jamiah shook his head. This was how people died in the movies. The idiots always had to *check it out*. Jamiah was too smart for that. But he was also too smart to believe this was some sort of horror movie. He tapped his bar against the makeshift door and waited to see if a deluge of spiders came pouring out—for which he was prepared to run. Or perhaps a rabid animal or a squatter lurked behind the secret passage.

"Hey! Better get the fuck outa my house." He used his toughest, deepest voice, which was trembling, but he hoped it wasn't obvious to whoever may have been listening.

Jamiah considered throwing on some shoes and a shirt before opening the door all the way, but instead of being a big baby about it, he pushed his fear aside and decided to peek in.

If they found him dead and shirtless in the morning, at least it was during a time in his life when he was in shape. He'd spent a lot of time doing pull-ups in his home gym, working away his dad-bod, as Alyssa called it. Even if he wasn't a dad, he was gaining all the physical characteristics as he entered his thirties. Jamiah shook off the vision of his own corpse on the floor, with investigators and the overly friendly neighbor looking on, as if they'd be talking about his physique.

"Screw it." He used the end of the bar to wedge it behind the door and pry it fully open. It creaked on aching, frail hinges, exposing a small two-by-two-foot closet. Aside from some webs in the corners, and a dusty old book propped on a ledge along the wall, the mini-closet was empty. The spider revealed itself, scurried along the floor, and then disappeared in a gap under the interior wall.

Jamiah shivered, and before he shut the makeshift door closed, he caught sight of a pentagram on the cover of the old book. He picked it up, wiping away the dust and got out of the claustrophobic space of the hidden closet.

Jamiah brought the book into the kitchen for a look under better lighting and laid it flat on the counter. On the leather cover, there was a dark crimson shape, but it wasn't a pentagram like he'd thought. Red paint flaked off in patches. A large outer circle did not contain a star in the middle. Rather, another center circle stood in its place with eight bent lines extending to the outer edge. Despite the worn-off bits, he could identify the shape as a crudely-drawn spider. He yanked his hand away from the drawing as if a real spider had touched his fingers. The sensation of it against his skin was enough to make him cringe.

He opened the book to see the deckled edges of a journal, each page filled with hand-written text. Some in black ink, and some in a similar deep red as the paint on the cover.

There were drawings of spiders and circles. Notes

about followers and the *Great Rising*. He flipped through without pausing on any one page. The entire book was packed with nonsense about spiders and worship. Definitely not a sex cult.

But a spider cult?

"Seriously?" Jamiah stopped flipping when he saw an image depicting a circle with eight people inside. They were drawn like spokes on a bike wheel, head to head, as if each person were a leg of the spider. In the center was a red flame. The text accompanying the drawing read:

Only the Chosen Eight shall deserve Her glory. They shall drink from her body the elixir of life, ignite the center flame, and only then shall the Chosen Eight become Arachnu's Great Rising.

"What the fuuuuck…" he whispered.

A journal full of spider-worshipping nonsense—the coming of the *Great Arachnu*—some kind of eight-legged horseman of the apocalypse or whatever.

He'd seen enough and pushed the book away from himself. His curtainless windows now felt like a threat. As if there were spider-cultists waiting outside, watching through the windows to see what he'd do. To see if he found their weird book.

From the windowsill, a wolf spider glared at him. Jamiah gasped, but then steadied himself. Another spider crept in through the cracked window and joined. Both standing side-by-side, measuring Jamiah up, decoding his movements. He reached for the aerosol can of bug spray and aimed, dusting them in a cloud of toxic fumes.

The spiders backed away, but instead of scurrying

out the window, or running for their lives choking on the spray, they stopped. Dead still while Jamiah sprayed them again, this time more directly. No twitching. No curling onto their backs in little spider fetal balls—not a single movement.

They froze for a few seconds, then rushed toward him. Both at the same time. Each spider leapt from the windowsill onto the counter's edge. Jamiah squealed in the highest pitch that had come out of his mouth since middle school.

He snagged the lighter from beside the gas stove and flicked a flame to life. Holding it at arm's reach, he sprayed the aerosol bug spray toward the spiders, creating a plume of fire. His fingers held steady to the depressor until both creatures were engulfed in flames. They dropped from the counter. Their crisp, charred bodies curled in on themselves.

The edge of the kitchen sink turned black, as did part of the cabinets below, but that was the worst of the damage. Fortunately, nothing else caught fire.

"Nope. Nope. Nope." He couldn't stay in this place one second longer. There were plenty of hotels in town, and plenty of contractors that could do the renovations… or maybe he'd simply admit defeat and sell the place to the next sorry son-of-a-bitch.

But he was done with this place.

As for the spider-cult book, he decided it should be turned into police. In case there was any truth to neighbor Dana's claims about all of them disappearing, the book may be evidence or something.

Jamiah left the spider carcasses on the floor and tucked the book under his arm, keeping his lighter and bug spray armed. He popped open the secret closet door and placed the book back where he'd found it—he wasn't sure if that's what the police would want, considering he'd already moved it, but it seemed like the right thing to do.

He balanced the book on the ledge along the back wall of the hidden closet, but the wall gave under the slightest pressure. His hands sank with the moving wall as the back of the closet swung open, creating another secret passage deeper into the house. He nearly tumbled into the pitch-dark space, but caught himself on the edge of the makeshift door frame. Cool, stagnant air rushed over him, like he'd opened an ancient vault. The opening did not lead to another closet, but a stairway going down. A basement—which his slab home was not supposed to have.

The sinkhole.

He grabbed his phone from his pocket and shone the flashlight into the space. Rickety wooden steps led down. Who the hell would build stairs into a sink hole? He took two steps down and bent over to get a look under the foundation slab.

The edge of the clay along the wall appeared smoothed and intentional. As if someone had turned the sinkhole into some sort of room. To his left, a wire ran along the clay wall. He followed it with his fingers until he reached a switch on the inside of the doorway. He flicked it, and an incandescent bulb buzzed to life below.

A soft yellow glow exposed a carpet of lumpy black

along the floor. Movement, like the entire floor was a wave rolling under the light. Jamiah's eyes quickly adjusted to the bright light to see thousands—maybe millions—of wolf spiders covering the floor. In the center of the room stood a table with a large pillar candle. The spiders cleared away, crawling over each other's bodies in a mass exodus of the glaring overhead bulb.

Jamiah's scream caught in his throat, and he turned quickly to get the hell out. As he did, the creaking old steps shifted underfoot. Along the frame of the makeshift door, spiders had gathered. Jamiah had no place to grab, so he tucked his arms in and tried to drive his body straight through, but the steps collapsed under his weight and he crashed down onto the undulating carpet of spiders.

A primal scream arose from his core and echoed off moving walls. The spiders continued their frantic crawl away from the center of the room, while Jamiah clamored to his feet, swatting his body and his head like he was on fire.

Then his body froze in terror. Every muscle seized. His visioned narrowed, like he might pass out. While his body wavered, spiders spread out from the center of the room, exposing the table under the pillar candle… and human figures. Eight bodies laid around the center.

The Chosen Eight must have drunk their deadly Kool-Aid elixir right here, in an attempt to bring their spider god to life. Eight corpses, months into decomposition. Skeletal frames peeked through mummified-looking flesh.

The sensation of hundreds of tiny legs on his thin pajama pants tore Jamiah from his petrified state, and he let out a scream. A swell of spiders climbed his legs. He dove for the bright green can of bug spray and blue lighter which lay on the floor where he'd fallen. Hairy legs brushed his hands as he gripped his life-saving weapons.

Despite the risk, he sprayed his own legs, causing some of the spiders to fall. Something took over. Survival instinct, he presumed. But he let rage consume his fear and he lashed out, stomping his bare feet on hundreds of hairy bodies. Exoskeletons crunched under the soft part of his feet.

The dilapidated staircase lay in pieces on the floor, so he'd have to jump and pull himself out. He threw bug spray flames at his exit. Tiny fiery corpses dropped, clearing his path. Behind, more rushed toward him, so Jamiah twisted back and swept the room with flames. He dusted fire across the surface of the moving carpet, across the bodies of the chosen eight, and incidentally, lighting the center pillar candle.

With the lighting of the wick, a single leg of the closest human corpse twitched. Then another. Their bodies jerked and trembled, inching toward each other, head-to-head beneath the table, until the table lifted and fell over, knocking the candle to the floor. The bodies connected, creating an abdomen of human heads and mummified faces. Each decrepit corpse creaked and snapped, contorting into a giant spider leg. All eight bodies moved together as one sentient being.

Jamiah twisted around to see Dana standing in the doorway above him.

"Oh my God! Are you okay?"

"Move!" Jamiah leapt, grabbing the edge of the foundation floor above him and pulled his body onto the landing. Dana backed up, stomping on spiders as they scurried out of the sinkhole.

"You've got a real infestation problem here!" She clutched a bottle of vodka in one hand.

Jamiah pushed past her. "Run!"

"Is that a fire down there?" Dana stayed behind to look. She froze in the doorway, unable to scream.

Jamiah rushed back to her, grabbed the bottle of vodka from her grip and threw it as hard as he could. It smashed below over remnant flames, and ignited into a fiery ball. The fire engulfed the creature. Gasping shrieks pierced the air—the cracked voices of eight burning corpses let out their final death cry.

Jamiah and Dana fled the house. Outside, he thrashed, smacking his body with rubber-like arms. "Are there any on me?"

"What the hell was that?" Dana stared at the house as it glowed orange with engulfing flames.

"Are there any on me?" He dropped to the ground, rolling in the grass.

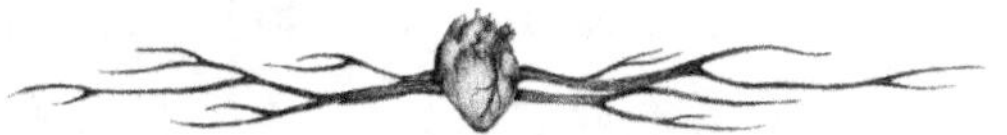

The spider house and its contents burned to the ground. While firefighters worked on extinguishing the last embers of the fire, Jamiah sat with Dana on the curb and called his wife, confessing the property was a wasted investment. Even her expected "I told you so" was a welcomed sound.

Eight charred bodies were recovered from the

blackened hole in the earth. And all but one item was destroyed. A fireman approached and handed him a leather-bound book pulled from the ash—the book telling the coming of Arachnu.

Behind him, another neighbor approached with a drink tray. "Thought you two could use my signature coffee. It's been a long night."

Jamiah accepted the cup and took a sip—pumpkin spice. His lip twitched. "I hate this fucking season."

THE GLASS LABYRINTH

In the off-season, the seaside town carried on its salty breeze the ghosts of Isaac Tripp's childhood memories. Stomping barefoot in the ocean, sunburns, salt-water taffy, and aggressive gulls swooping down for bits of French fries or funnel cake. But those glimpses of his past had been viewed through the naïve goggles of innocence for too long. Much like an ice cream cone on the beach, melting away and leaving nothing behind but sticky fingers and disappointment, so did Isaac's rosy picture of his childhood.

Looking back now as 35-year-old man, he recalled being alone most of these vacations. Mom and Dad would party all night, ensuring him he'd have fun with total control of the hotel TV. And during the day, while they nursed hangovers, he'd often get tired of waiting and venture to the beach by himself.

Gulls screeched, breaking Isaac from his memory, and an icy wind lashed across the shore, stirring up clumps of sea foam. Thick, snow-ladden clouds darkened. The sun must've already been setting behind them. Isaac bundled his coat tighter before turning his back to the ocean and toward the abandoned glass house attraction.

It was the one place he wanted to go when his parents brought him here on vacation over 20 years ago. While he roamed the boardwalk, exploring storefronts, he stopped before an all-glass façade with giant signage over double doors reading:

The Glass Labyrinth:
The most difficult maze in the universe!
Enter at your own risk.

Without a dime in his pocket, he rushed back to beg his father for money, but Dad wouldn't give it to him. He promised they'd go together before the vacation was over, but with each passing day, and each reminder, Dad kept making excuses.

On their last evening in town, Isaac begged with more passion than he'd ever begged for anything, and—since Mom and Dad were all partied out for the week—he took thirty minutes of his time to walk down the boardwalk with Isaac as the day wound down. A coral sunset sparkled atop crashing waves. Throngs of beachgoers turned to silhouettes against the light.

Issac could finally test his wits in *the hardest glass maze in the universe!* And he got to do this amazing thing with his father—with whom he rarely spent any time.

A twinge of disdain stirred in Isaac's belly as he recalled getting closer to the glass maze. Blue and red lights flashed out on the street and the boardwalk in front of the maze house was blocked by police tape.

"Sorry kiddo," Dad had said, with a hint of relief in his tone.

Isaac got closer, hoping the maze was still open. Dad hung back and lit a cigarette, leaning against the railing of the boardwalk to enjoy the view as the sun dipped below the horizon. "Probably a drug bust or something."

Isaac craned his neck around a crowd that had formed and ducked under elbows and purses to squeeze closer to the building, but at some point he found himself on the opposite side of the police tape in the alleyway that led to the street.

A side door was propped open with a cinderblock, and from it, the faint sound of a girl's voice cried, "Let me out." There was a sadness and desperation to the voice, and also distance—or perhaps muffled. Isaac knew he shouldn't have been on the other side of the police tape, but the alleyway was dark and empty and nobody even noticed he was in there, so he stayed in the shadow and eased closer to the door to get a look inside.

A long hallway stretched into the darkness of the glass maze. Soft string lights glowed along the ceiling, reflecting off glass walls that stretched into infinity. Inside, a teenage girl stood with two hands against a pane of glass. She had long black hair that draped over her shoulders like spilled ink. Isaac remembered thinking how pretty she was, but then he felt an ache in his chest. Panic and desperation were in her eyes. She begged silently for help, but Isaac froze, unsure what he should do.

"Hey kid!" a police officer from the street ducked under the yellow tape, but Isaac sprinted into the crowd before the cop could nab him. He squeezed through the people and found his Dad still leaning against the boardwalk railing with a smoke.

"People are saying someone died in there," Dad said, flicking ash from the cigarette into the sand. "Good thing we didn't go. Coulda been us!" Dad laughed and elbowed Isaac playfully.

Isaac had wanted to say something about the girl. He wanted to tell his dad that someone in there needed help, but he knew how that conversation would've went. Maybe he shouldn't have run away from the cop, but instead told the police there was a girl inside. He was just a kid, and he was too scared to fess up that he'd crossed the police tape.

He'd reasoned with himself that the cop in the alleyway would've seen her in there and helped. This is what he told himself all evening as he thought of how terrified and alone she looked. He wanted to sneak out and go down to the maze house, see if she still needed help. But, even as a kid, he knew it was pointless. That place was swarming with police and emergency vehicles. Someone had to have helped her…

Isaac shuddered against the wind and headed down the alleyway alongside the abandoned glass maze building and stood in front of the side emergency exit door just like he had done when he was a kid. There was no handle on the outside. No cinderblock nearby.

"I see I'm just in time!" A lanky man in a suit with no tie approached, extending a hand with a key dangling from a simple ring. "Nice to finally meet you."

The realtor bundled his jacket to the wind tunneling

through the alleyway. Isaac had bought the property sight-unseen just before his divorce from Carol. Months ago, she'd suggested a couple's therapy retreat to this town, and it inspired him to do a little digging to find out if the glass maze was still standing.

It'd always been there in the back of his mind. The desire to wander the maze, to lose himself in the halls of eternity…and she'd always been there too. The young girl with the spilled ink hair, asking a boy for help—and he ran away. She haunted his dreams from time to time. Nothing obsessive, but every few years, she'd be in his mind and he'd pour a drink to drown his regrets.

A quick search and Isaac had pulled up the run-down old beachfront amusement. It was for sale. Sold "as-is". A bargain for a beachfront business, so without even consulting with his wife, he'd bought it. Impulsive. Stupid. Inconsiderate. Carol called him a lot of things, and he couldn't disagree. It was irresponsible, but something inside of him insisted that he needed to have this building. He needed to go back.

Isaac wasn't stupid, though. He fully recognized that there was some underlying childhood trauma at work here. At the forefront of his mind, he felt guilty about the girl, but really—and his therapist agreed—he needed to take control of his own life. Reclaim the things he was never allowed to have, do the things he'd always been too scared to do. The girl from the maze haunted him over the years because of the compartmentalized trauma that Isaac needed to deal with.

The realtor unlocked the door which jingled a small

bell above his head. and they stepped behind glass walls into the foyer. All that was left to do was sign the official closing papers and it was all his. A dusty counter was directly in front of them, and the entrance to the maze was to the right. Around to the left, was access to the office behind the counter, the maze exit, and the restrooms.

"This place has had a few different owners over the years. They buy it with the intention of cleaning it up, but..." he gestured about the room. "...nobody ever opened for business, as far as I know."

"I wonder why not," Isaac said.

"It's gonna be a lot of work..." The fluorescent bulb overhead flickered and the realtor shrugged. "...a lot more than just elbow grease."

Isaac smirked. "You better hand me those closing papers before I change my mind."

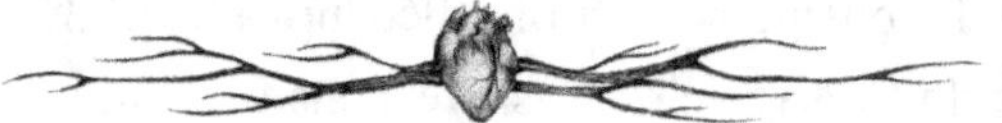

After the realtor left, Isaac kicked his feet up onto the office desk and popped the cork on the realtor's gifted bottle of cheap champagne. He thought this would feel different. He thought the ache in his chest would vanish when he finally reclaimed his biggest childhood disappointment, but all he felt was alone. The way he'd always felt.

Alone as a child on the beach. Alone as he entered his teenage years and grew angsty and distant from his parents. Alone when they threw up their arms and gave up on their kid, leaving him to navigate life on his own. They never abused him physically or verbally. They never left him without food, clothing, or shelter. He was taken care of only in the most basic sense, so he never complained about his upbringing much. It wasn't until his relationship with Carol took an epic nosedive that he realized he had some issues with personal relationships. Don't let them get close, and they can't disappoint you. Leave them before they can hurt you.

And now he drank shitty champagne alone in a dusty dump of a shack that needed more money for repairs than it was worth.

He closed his eyes and took a deep breath of dust motes, then expelled them in a violent cough. As his cough echoed off empty walls, the soft sound of a voice ricocheted in his head:

Let me out.

Isaac jumped, knocking his chair over and the bottle of champagne tipped.

"Shit." He grabbed the bottle and turned it upright. The foyer was draped in gray-blue twilight with the view of the beach filling the glass front. The voice had to have been in his head. He'd been thinking of that memory, and his mind was messing with him. Isaac searched for a rag to clean the mess as the trickle of champagne spilled over the edge of the desk and into a crate full of old newspapers.

As he pulled the yellowed papers out of the crate and placed them on the wet desktop to soak the spill, he noted they were dated over 20 years old.

Champagne absorbed through the old paper in seconds, dark spot expanding across a headline reading *Local Girl Dies in Maze.*

Without tearing the wet paper, he tried to read the

date—July…*something*…1998. It was around the time he'd visited with his family as a kid. He skimmed through the article—bits had faded, but he could make out most of it. Jessica Moore, a teenager with a history of heart problems and epilepsy, had died in the maze. Based on witness accounts, they speculated that Jessica sought refuge from bullies in the glass maze, where she suffered a grand-mal seizure and died from heart failure.

"Excuse me," a voice said.

Isaac whipped around to see a woman in his foyer, silhouetted against the windows.

"Uh…we're not open yet." He opened the office door and entered the foyer but it was empty. The front door was locked, deadbolt in place.

There was only one place she could've gone. Behind him, in the corner, the entrance of the maze was nothing but a black rectangle against chipped paint walls.

"You can't be in here!" he shouted into the void.

Isaac pried open the control panel beside the entrance and flipped the breaker. To his surprise, floor-to-ceiling glass panels lit up under the dim glow of string lights.

He peered deep into the maze, but he couldn't see anyone inside. The glass panels multiplied into the distance, vanishing into blackness.

"Miss?" His heart sped. "We're not open!" He took a step into the maze, skin awash in the glow. A childlike sensation of wonder surged through his veins, but it was quickly tempered when he heard a gentle, whimpering cry coming from deep within the labyrinth.

A lump in his throat swelled and made it difficult for

him to move.

The tiny incandescent bulbs along the ceiling blinked out and a voice carried through pitch-black halls. The voice fractured into incoherent sounds—consonants broke away from their words. They rapped at his ears, sending his neck hair to attention.

With outstretched hands, Isaac entered farther into the maze, turning at the first glass wall. "Hello?"

Lights flickered back to life to reveal a woman—maybe a teenager—sitting against a corner with her arms around her knees, rocking. Long black hair spilled over her face obscuring her identity.

A series of glass walls separated them, and Isaac maneuvered through until there was only a single panel between them. She sat tucked against a black wall.

Her name grew from the lump in his throat and lay heavy on his tongue. He couldn't believe it, but she was right in front of him. "Jessica Moore?" He grabbed the edge of the glass panel and moved to the other side, but she was gone.

Panic took control. It surged through his body. Nerves prickled into a frenzy. If he could sprint out of the maze, he would, but all he could do was fumble from one glass wall to another, frantic to get out.

He paused to get control of himself, to reel in the hysteria. He stood with his eyes closed, hands grasping the edges of a glass panel. He opened his eyes to see his anxious breaths had fogged the glass in front of him. After a few deep, calming breaths, he wiped away the fog to see the girl on the other side. She was on the floor, rigid body shaking violently. Vomit dribbled from her mouth. Unblinking eyes locked on Isaac.

A scream caught in his throat. He turned to run, but slammed face-first into a wall. He navigated through the labyrinth's turns and deceiving exits. Terror kept him moving, focused on getting out, but he'd lost his way.

Overhead lights flickered. Straight ahead, standing behind a sheet of glass, was the girl. She appeared this time exactly as she did all those years ago. Desperation in her eyes, something sad. This time, she reached toward him.

His chest heaved as an icy cold feeling encompassed his shoulder. The cold seeped through his muscles and extended into his chest, chilling his heart. His breath became a cloud of winter fog.

But as Isaac tried to swat her arm away, he realized it was only her reflection in front of him. Jessica's pale hand had grabbed him from behind.

"Let me out." Her voice was exactly as he remembered it decades ago.

Isaac broke away, crashing into glass walls, lights flickering. Ahead, the outline of a door finally came into sight. A red light reading *emergency exit only* gave him hope at getting out of his nightmare. He kept his hands in front of him, feeling his way through the maze until he reached the door. He worked the rusty deadbolt until it broke free and Isaac spilled onto the pavement in the alleyway. He folded in half and pulled in a life-saving breath of relief.

Heavy snowflakes fell around him, coating the

pavement. The sounds of waves crashing in the distance cut through the darkness of the night.

Let me out—her disembodied voice pleaded again between the sounds of waves.

Inside, down the hallway of glass, Jessica remained. She stood with hands against the window. The wind caught the heavy door and it began to blow shut. Her desperate eyes faded to disappointment, and she turned away, disappearing into the maze, alone.

Isaac, without thinking, stuck his foot in the door, keeping it from closing. He wanted to run more than anything. He wanted to believe he was hallucinating… that his childhood trauma was worse than he'd thought. He wanted to call for help—let someone else deal with this.

He huffed out a few sharp breaths, like preparing for a fight, then stepped back into the maze. He tread carefully down the hall of glass, heart beating so hard he thought it might stop. When he reached the glass panel, he turned to face the exit. Maybe if he waited for her, she'd come back to him. Or maybe she'd grab him with her icy grip and seize his heart.

"Hello?" His breath turned to fog.

The chill of a ghostly hand entered his palm. He drew in a breath and held it in his lungs. Without looking behind, he walked slowly toward the alleyway exit.

Her grip on his hand sent an icy ache deep into his bones as she followed. Isaac stepped outside, and a plume of fog poured onto the pavement. It swirled into the ghostly image of Jessica. Snowflakes fell through her apparition, and she stretched out translucent arms. Black hair did not move in the breeze. Her expression didn't change. Jessica's form drifted away from him toward the beach and dissipated in the glow of boardwalk lights, finally free from the maze.

Warm blood rushed back into Isaac's body, teeth chattering against the cold winter storm.

"Sorry it took me so long." He waved as she vanished into nothingness, leaving him alone once again.

DOGWOOD

The budding dogwood tree hadn't bloomed after Elijah's daughter went missing. He told his little girl the other day *they'll be in full bloom tomorrow…* only, tomorrow never came. Having not yet broken open, the pale white flowers remained trapped in incipient bloom, much like time had remained in stasis since Lei vanished.

The sweet scent of unblossomed flowers awaited release from its prison of closed buds while Elijah sat beneath on the swing he'd hung for his daughter. The swing was meant to be one he'd push her on every day. He imagined her smile reaching the sky. The aged dogwood tree would grow with her. The swing would be a safe haven for his little girl. Maybe one day, when she was older, the swing would witness young love in blossom— maybe she'd experience her first kiss under its boughs. As Lei grew up in his mind, the dogwood would be in full bloom overhead. Lei would wear a white, flowy gown for a wedding at home, never outgrowing the swing which Daddy had built when she was only six years old.

Her absence filled his chest until he couldn't breathe. Another unsuccessful day of searching left him exhausted and furious that he failed her. Police would be back in the morning to do another search of the surrounding area, this time with townspeople for a comb of the woods. As twilight devoured the day, Elijah went into his kitchen, where the walls were half-painted yellow. Lei picked the color. Plastic sheets covered the floor to catch splatters. It crinkled underfoot.

A day and a half ago, Elijah had asked Lei to play outside when the fumes in the house became overbearing. He painted, watching from the kitchen window as she made a cape with a stolen segment of painter's plastic. She tucked it in the back of her shirt collar and swung as high as she could go, her makeshift cape billowed behind her. The next thing he recalled, he'd regret for eternity.

"Daddy!"

"Stay outside, sweetie. It's stinky in here." He met her at the front door.

"I saw a bunny!"

"Wow! A bunny, huh?" Elijah took a seat on the porch bench, resting his head against the wall. "You'll probably see a lot of bunnies now that we live in the country."

"I think it lives in there." She pointed to the woods between a thicket of thorns and another younger dogwood tree on the verge of blooming.

"Mhmm…" Elijah rested his eyes for a moment.

It was just a moment. He had no intention of sleeping. Hell, if he thought he needed to rest, he would've made Lei come inside first. At least thirty minutes had passed since he shut his eyes. Maybe more, as he didn't recall checking the clock when he'd stopped painting.

Lei was gone.

The last thirty-six hours were a nightmare from which he couldn't seem to wake. He screamed for her until his voice stripped raw. Thorny brush had carved up his flesh as he ripped through the woods, checking every thicket, every place where she might be hiding. There were police and search dogs and…

…and nothing.

Now, as the day came to an end, Elijah stood gazing out the window at the swing which hung without a sway, stiff as a sculpture beneath the dogwood that refused to bloom.

He closed his eyes and focused on hope—on the chance that she'd wandered off and was hiding in some thicket with those bunnies she must've chased after. Of course, there were other terrible possibilities scratching at his brain. Things he tried not to think about. Things that happen to little girls and turn otherwise docile parents into raging knots of fury. When his mind went to those places, his fists turned to white-knuckled balls. The anger was so overwhelming he felt like he might explode. Everything hurt so much, he wished he would explode into a million pieces so he couldn't feel the pain.

Fortunately, the police didn't pick up on any signs of foul play. There were only two sets of footprints on the property—Lei's and Elijah's.

Her purple sparkly sneakers left zig-zagging footprints in the soft, spring earth. Beyond the edge of the yard, pine straw padded the forest floor, creating a carpet that tiny footsteps could not disturb. It was a dead trail.

Elijah leaned against the kitchen sink, squeezing the edge, and squeezing tears from his closed eyes. He caught control of his gasping breath and lifted his head. Out the window over the sink, someone stood by the dogwood swing.

It was a small figure, cloaked like a bedsheet ghost. A black circle was cut out for a mouth. It stood inflexible to the breeze as if it'd been ironed stiff with starch. There was a translucence to the sheet, but it was too dark to make out who was underneath.

Elijah froze, afraid to blink. Afraid to lose sight of her. In the moment of silence between heartbeats, he wondered if it was possible. Maybe she'd been hiding and found her way home. Or maybe it was some kid playing a practical joke.

Headlights shone at the end of his gravel driveway as the sheriff pulled in. Elijah ran through his house, out the front door, and down the steps toward the dogwood tree. The little person dressed as a ghost was gone. The swing swayed but there was no perceptible breeze.

The headlights cut off and the sheriff stepped out of the vehicle.

"There was someone here. A kid!" Elijah scanned the yard, hoping to bring her back into sight.

"When?"

"Just now."

The sheriff helped Elijah check the perimeter of the property, all the way down to the pond, but they found nothing.

"I'm telling you, I saw it."

"Do you think it was her?"

"I…" Elijah tried to make sense of it. There'd be no reason for Lei to play games. By now, she'd be scared and hungry. "I don't know. But I know I saw *someone*."

The sheriff scratched his head. "I'll go talk to the Reiners down the road and make sure Danny ain't playing pranks."

Elijah nodded, heart finally settling back into his chest. He rubbed his face.

The sheriff nodded. "You should try to get some sleep."

"I need to keep looking. I can't just go to sleep."

"Ain't gonna see much out there at night. Those woods are black as pitch. Tomorrow, a crew will be here to help look for your little girl…and to dredge the pond."

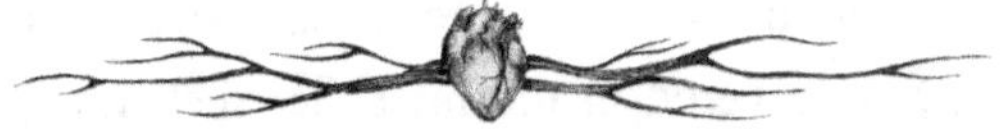

Elijah sat on the porch all night, in and out of consciousness. The light was on as a beacon to lure Lei home. He closed his eyes and dreamt of the pond. A rowboat floated on a sea of dogwood petals. The harder he searched for his little girl, the deeper his boat sank, until finally, he was drowning in the petals. As he inhaled deeply before going under, the stiff-sheeted ghost appeared above him. Its eyes were no more than blurred suggestions over its black oval mouth.

Elijah startled awake to a gray-blue, predawn world. He'd slept on the porch all night and woke to a fog so thick, it swallowed the forest. It clung to his clothes, chilling his skin.

At the edge of the yard, where Lei had pointed toward the bunny's path, a solemn figure stood—the sheet ghost kid.

"Hey!" Elijah leapt to his feet. "Do you think this is funny?!" he squinted through the haze, but the kid in the sheet faded away.

"Hey!" He jogged down the porch steps toward the edge of the forest. His daughter's footsteps were marked off with yellow tape. He stepped around the evidence toward the younger dogwood at the edge of the woods. Unlike the tree with the swing that refused to flower, this dogwood had already bloomed to life.

A rustling of brush drew his eyes to his feet where a small wild rabbit took off, startled by Elijah's presence. As it disappeared between fog-choked pines and scattered blooming dogwoods in the forest, the sheet ghost figure returned. She hovered in the mist, her feet devoured by the clouded earth. Her mouth was a gaping maw as if calling for help.

Every fatherly instinct told him this was how he'd find his girl. If he followed, he'd find her. But every time he moved toward it, it vanished. And when he thought he had traveled too far, and had no idea where he was, she'd appear again, showing him the way. He must have walked for an hour or more when something rational took over.

He was wasting time—figments of his imagination. Stress. Elijah didn't understand if he was going insane or if some kid was screwing with him, but it didn't matter.

He was chasing ghosts when he could be back home awaiting the search party.

The sun had risen, breaking gently through patchy clouds and fog. Elijah stood in a grove of fully bloomed dogwoods, ready to turn back. The soil was soft and coated in a layer of newly-fallen petals. His boots sank slightly into the mud and he wished the earth would just swallow him completely. He could sink into the dirt until he couldn't breathe—maybe it's what he deserved for falling asleep.

The apparition appeared again. The starchy fabric seemed to move now—only it wasn't like bedsheet fabric. Orange light from the rising sun shone upon the figure. The material reflected the light. The figure raised an arm as if pointing toward a thick patch of greenery, then ducked beneath what looked like a hedgerow.

Elijah headed toward it and spotted small footprints in the dried mud. Little zig-zaggy sneaker prints.

"Lei!"

The hedgerow was a section of chain link fence overgrown with vines and weeds. The sound of tires on pavement grew in the distance. He stood at attention, seeking the source beyond the fence. About a hundred yards away, through dense trees, he could spot a vehicle driving by.

Elijah ducked through the opening in the fence. On the other side lay the ruins of an old foundation. Beyond the rubble of concrete and cinderblock, there was a small oval pond with an oddly symmetrical shape. It was an old swimming pool, devoured by nature and time. Black, stagnant water filled the pool. Lily pads floated at the surface. The cement surrounding it was cracked and coated with moss. Weeds and thorny brush had invaded the edges, spilling into the water.

Tangled in the thorns, there was a wadded segment of painter's plastic. Stiff and clean, it appeared the trash had not been there long.

Elijah eased around the edge of the black pool. A prickly mass of brush was ensnared in the plastic. He reached into the prickly vines. Thorny, gnashing teeth ripped at his flesh as he tugged on the plastic.

It twisted and tiny, purple sneakers floated to the surface.

The plastic sheet which had been a cape for Lei shrouded her head. Tangles of thorns pinned the plastic sheet to her body. Through the translucence, Lei's mouth was wide open in a final gasp for life-saving breath which never came.

He hadn't seen the sheet ghost since he found her body. After the funeral, Elijah sat on his daughter's swing. He was a statue, forever imprisoned in this moment of grief. A breeze rustled the leaves overhead and soft white petals floated away. He hadn't even noticed the tree had finally bloomed. He'd missed it, and now the flowers would fall to the earth. Spring did not bring forth life and new growth. Instead, spring brought the ephemeral beauty and death of the dogwood.

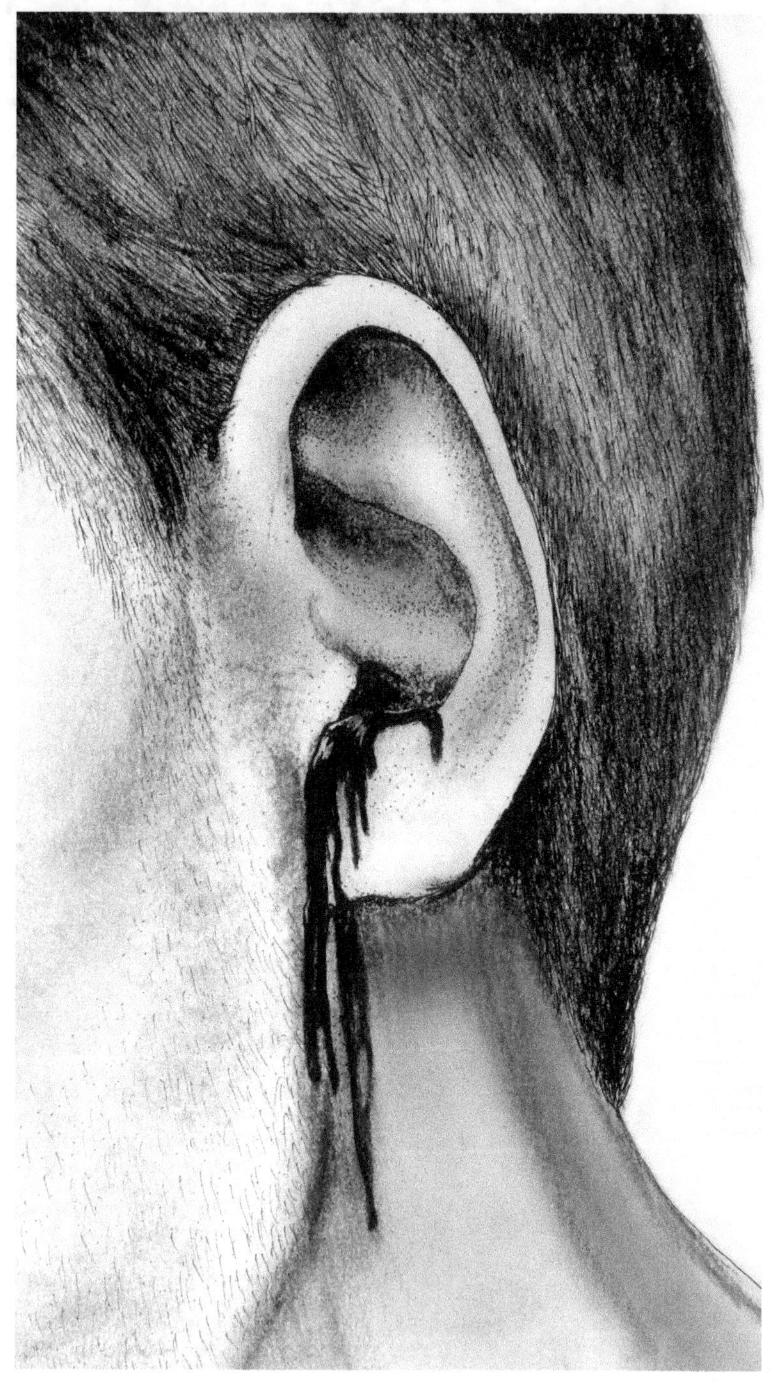

SENSORY DEPRIVATION

The cold is a sinister thing. Kind of like a woman's love, in my opinion. It creeps into weaknesses in my cabin. It slips down the chimney into the place where it should be the warmest. It invades my home, seeps through my coat and chills me to the bone. I thought I'd protected myself with insulation, a barrier wall around my heart to keep her chilled fingers from grabbing hold and squeezing, but she found a way in anyway.

The snowstorm came early. So did her untimely death.

Rachel's body lay like a board in my arms. Rigor Mortis set in shortly after the stench of death had filled the cabin. My secluded, off-the-grid sanctuary. The place I bring my loves to share the sweet bliss that develops in a relationship only when a couple can break away from society and be alone together. When there is nobody else around to see, to hear… *to touch.*

As I hold her lifeless form in my arms, I dream about what her warm body would have felt like pressed against mine. But this daydream does not bring comfort. Instead, a shiver skitters through my veins like the bitter cold of winter—she's inside, clawing her way toward my heart.

Pregnant clouds spill heavy snow over the mountainside. The ground is frozen beneath, and there's no way off this mountain until the storm subsides. This was not how it was supposed to be. The plan was to be snowed in together for the winter. Let her see how magical things could be if given the chance to be together, totally and completely immersed in each other's company. I'd imagined warm flesh and flushed skin by the fire, but now her lips match the color of the smokey blue clouds overhead. Her body is as cold as her grave—a temporary ice-grave dug into the snow beside the cabin, at least until I can bury her properly.

Her eyes are distant dull orbs, devoid of the life I'd seen in them when we first met. They were bright, reflecting trust and innocence—the way a woman should look at her man, in my opinion. Now they are vacant. All life, all prospects for love and affection have evaporated, sucked into the sky… only to fall back to earth as the sorrow-laden snowflakes I use to bury her.

I lean the shovel against the woodpile with the other tools, and head into the cabin, dreading the next few days of loneliness. From the tattered green loveseat, I sit, reaching the poker into the woodstove to stoke the flames. A brief surge of heat helps dry the tears from my face. My heart aches in the confinement of solitude. I wish I could hear her voice once again.

White-out conditions blur the landscape beyond the windows. The snow blows sideways, wind howls over the woodstove chimney like a banshee. It screams. A screaming reminiscent of Rachel's last cries. Cries I couldn't silence, no matter how much I tried to calm her. Cries that turned to cursing then to violent thrashing.

"Please don't—"

I shouldn't have pushed her.

If I had been patient with her, she wouldn't have asked to leave. And if I didn't get so angry, she never would have hit her head on the corner of the wood stove.

The incessant howling of wind carries down the chimney pipe in her voice. A steady shriek which I can't unhear. I lay on the couch, closing my eyes, covering my ears, but she continues to cry. It's unbearable.

"Shut up!" I bang against the pipe, but she keeps screaming…screaming…screaming.

Her voice thrusts down the chimney on a gust of wind, extinguishing flames.

Reigniting the fire is no easy task as an icy breeze pours from the stove. The cold reaches its tendrils into my home. The hot chimney should melt the snow on its way down, but a few flakes blow from the fireplace onto my skin. The frosty touch reminds me of her. It raises gooseflesh and I back away, reaching for a flannel hanging by the door.

The screaming won't cease. Hours pass with my hands pressed against my ears. I curl on the loveseat with a pillow over my head. And even though I've managed to start the fire, and the winds have seemed to slow, her voice still cries in my head, and her icy touch chills me to the bone.

I shiver. Teeth chattering. Ears aching at the sound of her cries.

More hours pass and the sky grows dark. She haunts my night. Screaming. Screaming. Screaming.

I should never have chosen her. I was too eager, too desperate. I'm smarter than this, but I succumbed to her bewitchment and wasn't thinking clearly. Now her banshee screams will not allow me a moment of peace.

By morning, her cries continue to ring in my ears. An insufferable tinnitus of screaming. No matter what I do, she is in my head. Never speaking a word. Never giving a piece of her mind. Only screaming.

Eyes bloodshot, face scruffy with a day's worth of growth, I stick a finger inside my ear to shake her free, but she persists.

"Shut up!" Tears drench my cheeks.

On the coffee table, I'd laid out a crossword puzzle and pencil for morning activities. The pencil's eraser may fit into my ear canal. It begs for relief. Perhaps if I gently insert, I can erase her out of my ear drums. Or better yet, maybe the sharpened tip could etch out her voice. Puncture a hole in the membrane to release her from my mind.

The graphite point slides into my canal and my eye spasms involuntarily. It catches, pencil wedged into the ear, but it's not far enough. Her screaming persists, and so do I.

I push deeper and graphite makes contact with the ear drum, invoking a gag reflex. My eye twitches, jaw collapses, and my mouth hangs agape with the sensation, but her voice only gets louder.

"Get out!" My palm pounds the end of pencil eraser. A clap of thunder in my head releases the witch from my mind. Her shriek flies away and sharp, searing pain fills the right side of my head. But her wails are still lodged in the other ear. Before I lose the nerve, I draw the pencil from my ear, and glide it into the opposite canal. I am not gentle or slow to act this time. I thrust it quickly and another shockwave in my head signals I've punctured the drum.

I pull the pencil and a flood of fluid fills both canals.

Rachel still screams, but she is muffled, diffuse. A brief moment of relief washes over me… but then vertigo takes over.

I can't find balance. The room pulls to one side, keeping me from staying on course to the kitchen. The cabin rocks like a ship on stormy water. I stagger, bumping against the kitchen table, but I find my way to the counter's edge and hold steady. Either vertigo or the pain sends my stomach upside down, and vomit ejects into the sink. After I've emptied my stomach's contents, I try to focus on something distant.

Outside, the storm has let up slightly. The worst of the blizzard may be over, but the sky continues to shake a gentle flurry from its grip. The soft downward motion of snowflakes against the blanket of white sways with my vision. Back and forth. I close my eyes to cut off the stimulation, but when my vision goes black, her voice returns. Breaking through blood-filled ears, it pierces the fluid and crawls into my head… Screaming. Screaming.

Screaming.

When I open my eyes, her face is in the window. Eyes wide. Mouth open to scream, she's there in the shadowy spaces between snowflakes. A rippling mirage. The sight of her sends me falling backward onto crepitating floorboards. Once I scramble to my feet, she is gone. I can't shake the image of her face… and now the screaming… the screaming is different. It's no longer muffled by my ears, but rather by the walls of the cabin.

There is no mistaking what I saw.

The door doesn't open easily. At least a foot of snow has drifted onto the porch, blocking the door. I throw a shoulder against the old wood and force it open. I am blasted by the return of her howling cries. They snake into my ears again as I step off the porch. Trudging waist-deep, I push mounds of snow out of the way and high-stepping to the side of the cabin where I'd buried Rachel the day before.

I need to know she's still there. I need to know I'm not imagining it all. So I dig. With bare hands I throw snow, determined to find her lying peacefully asleep. But the longer I dig, my hands become numb. I fight the invasive cold. I fight the screaming in my head and the visions of her out of the corner of my eyes, and I dig. The world shifts—or maybe it's vertigo pulling me to the side—but I keep focused on finding her body.

My lips are so cold I can't feel them anymore. Ice bites my fingertips. Snow has melted through my jeans, leaving my legs soaking wet. I shovel until I can't anymore…

Her body is gone, but her voice remains. A constant

shriek. An unyielding reminder of her disapproval.

I collapse to my knees in the snow, defeated. Begging for relief from her haunting squall.

In the distance, a figure looms near the tree line. I know there to be a copse of newly sprouted pines over there. And now a woman's silhouette takes shape. She comes into focus, even though my world still rocks back and forth. Fire-red hair is a stark contrast to the bright green of the young saplings.

It's not Rachel, though. This one's name was Isabelle. She was the last woman I loved. The last woman, before Rachel, whom I brought to this cabin. She stayed with me for weeks before her body gave up. Weeks! I was supposed to have weeks with my sweet Rachel.

The copse of trees is difficult to stay focused on as the world spins, lurching side to side. Isabelle's ghostly form lures me to her, her voice joins with Rachel's in my mind.

I set the shovel aside and pull the woodcutting axe from under a layer of snow. I must find them, stop them somehow.

I trek across the field toward the patch of woods where Isabelle had been buried in the soft summer soil. Where Rachel would have been laid to rest if she'd lasted until spring.

An ocean of snow must be crossed to get to her. With each step closer, her image grows more distant, but their screams intensify.

I near the copse of pine saplings where the ground snow isn't as thick. The surrounding towering evergreens have caught much of the snowfall. Here, to the right of an exposed granite boulder, is where Isabelle should lie. But she can't be in her grave because I see her a hundred yards up the mountain. She stands with Rachel, side by side, beyond the columns of trees. Their eyes are black and their jaws are unhinged to gaping maws. Together, they stand screaming—voices as loud as if they had crawled into my ears.

I ready the axe and scrabble up the mountainside along slick, icy rock and deep patches of snow. Each time I arrive where they'd been standing, they are gone… farther up the mountain. So, I follow. Balance fails me. The muffled blub-blub of my pulse in my head lays a beat for their soprano howls.

Glacial cold is inside me. Teeth chatter. Aching joints shiver. Stabbing needlelike pain in my toes. I need a second to rest. A second to catch my breath because the cold air is like glass shards in my lungs.

A pile of boulders creates a cave where the women were last sighted. I recognize this cave. I've been here once before.

They've led me back to *her.* To Janette. My very first love. I'll never forget the day I lay with her beneath the boulder pile. She trembled, hands shaking while they cupped my cheek. Tears filled her eyes. The poor thing was frightened.

The spiky pain in my toes is gone. In fact, all sensation below the knees has vanished too. Weak legs carry me to the cave, and as I enter, my legs give out and I collapse to the cave floor. And the screaming finally stops.

"Thank you!" I try to raise my hands in praise, but

they refuse to lift above my waist. I drop to my elbows, and give up on the fight to stay upright. I lie down on my side, in the same place where I held Janette for the last time. And the place where I'd buried her.

Her fears back then did not manifest as screams. No. Janette placed her fragile hands against my face and whimpered, "Please, don't." The hitch in her voice reverberates through my body.

Please don't. So polite…the way a woman should be, in my opinion.

As the image of her face returns to my memory, the faces of the other women close in on the safety of my cave.

Angry, ruthless faces shriek into the cave, sending violent shockwaves through my body. I close my eyes but their images are burned into my retinae. They're no longer scared, timid women. They are vengeful and full of hate.

The cold, hard ground between Janette's body and mine offers no comfort as I squeeze my lids shut. Icy frost permeates, stabbing crystals into my eyes. Kaleidoscope visions of the women I loved…the women I hurt.

I don't know how much time has passed, but it's getting dark.

Three women howl in my head. The world continues to spin.

I want to say Get out of my head, but my lips struggle to form words. If I could lift the axe, I'd cut out my eyes, but my hands have frozen.

I'm sorry. But my apologies feel empty, desperate.

Insincere. And if I know it, then surely they do as well.

Ice glazes my eyeballs and I am blinded, clinging to the earth, which rocks unsteady, swaying beneath me. I can see and feel nothing of this world anymore. All that remains is the sound of their screams, the memory of their faces, and now…the chill of their touch.

Icicle fingers crawl along my neck, glide across my jaw like a glacier. She cups my cheek. These fingers don't caress, but freeze. Bitter, hard touches, killing flesh as she traverses my skin. Her touch invades my flesh, and digs inward to my bloodstream. Icy crystals snake through veins to my chest, seizing.

All I want to do is scream, but my body is frozen solid.

As the cold permeates deep, it shatters bone, crushes my heart…squeezing, squeezing, squeezing…

Before I am forever entombed in her icy grip, I beg… "Please don't."

But I don't deserve their mercy, so I cower in eternal icy petrification with no other sensation but their fury… screaming. screaming. screaming.

BLOOD BOGGED

Stalactites of clotted blood hung from the mesh hammock. The nylon conformed to Erin's body, hugging her as she woke to another morning massacre beneath her. Blood had collected on the floor overnight, dripping between the netting and congealing on the small bedroom floor. The room had filled wall to wall, corner to corner. An ankle-deep layer of blood poured out of her body overnight. She twisted her head to look between the hammock's webbing. There was considerably less than the days before. The sound of gushing fluids had ceased.

Maybe it's finally over.

Erin's heart sped at the prospect of relief. Weeks of torrential menstrual bleeding finally came to an end.

Dried blood crusted her forearms to the hammock. She peeled them free and dusted brown flakes from her arm hair. The nylon cleaved to her skin. She ripped one leg free, yanking peach fuzz from the back of her leg.

Sweat dripped from her brow and fell to the decaying pomegranate carpet of gore below.

Something feels wrong.

Feverish, she dangled her free leg over the edge. An ache in her abdomen sent a wave of nausea through her body. Shaking hands reached for her cramping belly. A distended abdomen, so full she'd think she was seven months pregnant if she didn't know any better. The fluid inside pressed against her stomach and pushed the contents up her throat.

Erin rolled to her side and retched.

Last night's soup noodles ejected, splattering like worms onto the burgundy-colored cruor underneath. The muscle spasms from vomiting forced pressure below and broke free the clotted sluice between her legs.

Blood burst forth. A deluge of crimson rushed from her vagina. A sudden shift in pressure in her abdomen made her stomach drop. She could've puked again, but she choked it back and sat at the edge of the hammock. Bare feet dangled above the hardening red sea as fresh waves of scarlet butchery drained from her uterus.

Erin had been bleeding several gallons per hour, non-stop for two weeks. A biblical-level flow that she imagined would drown the world if it didn't stop. Her uterus contracted and debilitating cramps doubled her over. Perspiration soaked her dark hair as well as the towel she had wrapped herself with before going to bed. She didn't bother wearing clothes anymore. Cracked, dehydrated lips begged for more water. She couldn't get enough lately.

Light-headed and queasy, Erin took steady breaths to calm her nerves. The build-up of fluid in her body overnight may have had a toxic effect, or…

Is this it? Am I finally dying?

Tears threatened to fall as she considered the relief death could bring. It was inexplicable why she hadn't died already with so much blood loss. Erin had laid in the hospital for days as doctors tried to figure it out. Incomprehensible medical terms flew around the room between consulting experts, but none of the diagnoses made sense. As only a freshman biology major, Erin didn't have the education to figure out what they were talking about. Those words fluttered around in her head—rapid platelet regeneration, myeloma, polyceth-something, too much plasma…cancer? Doctors tossed any and all possibilities into the pool of ideas, but nothing came back positive. Erin's condition was a mystery.

They dug into her medical history, asking about her parents, about her sex life. The bleeding had started shortly after she had intercourse with a man, but since it was technically consensual, it didn't concern the doctors. She'd been sexually abused as a young child, but sharing that information was more invasive than any test they could do.

She wished someone could be with her now. Her parents had been out of her life for three years. And Sam wouldn't answer her calls. Not that she cared to speak with him. The meretricious nature of their relationship was toxic, and somehow—even though doctors didn't agree—Sam was responsible for her suffering.

Sweat clung to her skin, dampening the caked blood on her back and thighs, Erin eased her feet to the floor.

Toes dipped into the gelatinous muck and found the floor.

It's just like walking in Jello. Her daily attempts to convince herself that wading through ankle-deep decaying period blood wasn't disgusting proved futile.

Her abdomen retracted back to its normal size after expelling the build up of blood that had accumulated overnight. Her belly was back to mildly swollen—no more bloated than any other period. But the sickness, lightheadedness, and fever remained. Chills skittered across damp skin. She wrapped her hands around the dust mop in the corner and began her first task of the day, the first task every day.

Flowing like a hydrant, Erin had grown accustomed to walking with her legs apart…almost like a bad impersonation of a cowboy. She'd even tried having some fun with it, pretending to be in the wild west, but it wasn't funny. Nothing was fun anymore.

She pushed the old coagulated blood out of the bedroom and into a square hall space only large enough for two people to stand. To the right, sat a tiny bathroom. To the left was the basement, concealed in shadow.

Erin held her breath in anticipation of the stench as she opened the basement door. Erin broke into the cozy one-bedroom cabin for sanctuary last week. She wondered if it was smart to come to this place. She wondered if she could even call herself *smart* anymore. Maybe it was nobody's fault but her own.

Congealed blood and sloughed tissue piled into a jelly clump and she shoved it into the blackness of the basement with the rest of it. All week long, every morning, she mopped the butchery out of sight, launching it down the rickety wooden steps. A few days after arriving, the curdled heap of menstrual matter nearly reached the seven-foot ceiling, Erin had to navigate down the wobbly steps to knock the heaping pile down. To spread it out so there'd be room to shove in more. The necrotic, metallic stench of aging gore stung her nostrils. The old blood and bodily tissue had drawn flies and maggots. They buzzed and wriggled on the surface, feasting and fucking in her misery.

Erin was tired from mopping. Weakness took over and she leaned on the mop handle, staring into the black basement. The lake was inches from the ceiling and it'd only be a matter of another day or two before it would overflow, encroaching into the living space.

Stains and sticky remnant smears covered the cabin floors. Soon, she wouldn't be able to stay here any longer.

Only two termite-ridden wooden steps were visible above the surface level. She placed a foot carefully onto the first step. The staircase wavered under her weight. The second step sat level with the blood. As she used her arms to anchor herself to the walls, she stepped down. Fresh waves poured from her, adding a layer of wet fluid on top of the solidified mass, blanketing her feet. If she hunched down, she might've been able to see beneath the edge of the basement's ceiling. Perhaps there'd be room to move some of the heaping clumps toward the back and make space for more.

But as she attempted to bend, the staircase sank. Her knees buckled and Erin plunged into the gelatinous pool of rot. She twisted, grabbing the edge of the floor with one hand. Toes reached for the wood of the staircase, but it was gone, sunken too deep to find. The bare skin of her legs brushed against knots of mucilaginous muck. Her free hand pushed down on the coagulated top layer to get leverage, but it sank.

She tried to pull herself free, but with each movement of her feet, the suction of the bog pulled her deeper.

Thick, acrid aroma punched her nose and permeated her mouth. The rotting menstrual air lay heavy on her tongue. She gagged, dry-heaving, but nothing came up.

Erin calmed her racing heart and tried to think rationally.

She fortified her grip by swinging her elbow up so her left arm was solid on the floor. After wiggling her other hand free, she gripped her fingers around the door frame molding. Red fingerprints smeared eggshell paint.

Pulling her knees up only forced her deeper into the pit of quicksand blood, so she took a few calming breaths. As her feet dangled in the muck, the continuous flow between her legs created a puddle of viscous liquid. It filled a space around her calves. Fresh blood pooled around her knees, then her hips, creating a pocket. Free of the thick substance, she kicked her legs and launched herself upward. Erin hoisted her body out of the mire, losing her towel.

Naked and coated in a layer of decomposing period blood, Erin curled on the floor, arms squeezing her body. Guttural sobs burst from her core. With every gut-wrenching cry for help, her uterus erupted with explosive floods.

Erin crawled into the bathroom directly across from the basement door, a red trail behind her. Jellied remains stuck under her hands and knees, clinging in strings as she lifted each limb. Daylight shone through the shower window like Heaven's light calling her home.

The cool porcelain tub offered relief to her feverish body. Matted hair loosened as stiffened blood broke free. Shower water rained down as she lay alone, broken and lost.

She'd tried sleeping here the first couple of days, but she woke to a clotted drain and her body submerged neck-deep in an overflowing tub of blood.

Almost as fast as the blood made its exodus from her uterus, shower water rinsed it away. Clots and black tissue washed from between her legs. They gathered at the drain.

Erin mustered the strength to stand and washed away the dried clumps. Shampoo broke away the filth. Water ran pink, but the drain soon clogged and the fluid around her ankles turned red once again.

If only for a moment, she relished in the feeling of cleanliness. In the hospital, she had a team of people keeping up with her mess. They recorded that she bled four thousand gallons in just two days. Enough to fill a small backyard swimming pool. They transferred her to a locker room shower, where she could bleed freely, but didn't know what to do with her. Nurses and doctors whispered from behind the curtain. She was a lost cause. A burden. Maybe even cursed, if she believed in those kinds of things.

Guilt crept into her head and took over. Maybe if the doctors had all the information about her history, they could've helped her. But she couldn't seem to come forth and tell them what Sam had done. She wouldn't give his name, so she believed she had nobody to blame but herself.

Ashamed and embarrassed, Erin had run from the hospital. Blood-soaked pants dripped down the hallway as nurses raced after her. She sprinted to the parking lot to her car and took off.

A two-hour drive to the mountains. She'd cracked the door periodically to release the fluid collecting at her feet. It was the only place she could think to go. Sam's cabin. He had taken her there months earlier. They talked about science and biology. They laughed hysterically. They *loved*. He professed his feelings and insisted they must be soul mates, and Erin was naïve enough to believe him. At 42 years old, Sam was an unorthodox choice for an 18-year-old, but she considered herself mature for her age. Not like the other girls at school, not like Terra from her bio class with her incessant whining about shoes. Sam claimed to have seen something different in Erin.

She should've known better, because after the bleeding started, Sam ignored all of her calls. And for some reason, she protected their secret affair, protected his supposed *good* name.

The cabin was secluded. When she pulled up the gravel driveway over a week ago, Erin decided she would spend her last days here…there couldn't be many left.

Erin stepped out of the shower and sat on the edge

of the tub, allowing herself to drain into the basin. She brushed her hair until crippling cramps bent her in half.

She didn't want to die in this cabin. She didn't want to die at all, not for *his* secret. Realization climbed into her head and convinced her she needed help. She'd need to go back to the hospital.

The last remaining towel smelled musty. She wrapped it around her clean-for-now body.

What Sam did was inexcusable. He was a master of lies. His only goal was to bed the young freshman. She knew it deep down all along, but she wanted so badly to have someone good in her life. Someone who loved her.

Sitting at the edge of the tub, Erin rested her elbows on her knees. She recalled Sam's touch. Romantic kisses and love-making in his office, at his cabin, under the stars… She slept with Sam too many times to count.

Until she discovered he was married. Sam claimed he was unhappy and in the process of a divorce. Either way, Erin wanted out.

Sam had locked Erin in his office and backed her into a corner. He smiled. "I'm not done with you."

His words echo in her head as if he was standing right beside her.

I'm not done with you.

Blackmail was a powerful tool and he wielded it with expert precision. Looking back, she could have said *No*. She could have left her professor's office and reported him. But it all happened so fast. He said he'd accuse her of plagiarism—get her kicked out of school, scholarship stripped away—if she didn't submit to him right then. In the dim light of his after-hours office, she believed every word.

She consented. She let him touch her against her will, and it broke her. That night, she had gone home and started her period. Her body purged the disgusting remnants of his toxicity—of all the toxicity from over the years—but there was far too much to fully expel.

As the days went by, she hated herself less, and *him* more.

He should have known better.

Tires crunched the gravel out front. Erin stepped back into the shower to get a look out the window.

It was Sam's Suburu pulling up the drive. When the vehicle stopped, Terra from her bio class climbed from the passenger seat, staring at the ground beside Erin's Camry—blood stains dried to the gravel and trailed to the cabin.

Terra gasped. Her muffled voice was almost audible from inside.

A flutter of rage rumbled within Erin as Sam walked around the front of his car and placed a hand on Terra's back. He looked toward the cabin, knowing Erin was inside.

Erin sank away from the window. Her pulse went murky with anticipation of his reaction.

"Go back down the hill until you get a signal. Call the police."

Terra took the keys and peeled out, kicking up gravel as she disappeared down the drive.

Sam approached the porch.

Erin inhaled a deep breath and tightened the beige towel around her body. Time to confront him.

You can do this.

She stepped onto the floor. The slippery tile threw her off-balance. Erin crashed forward. The right side of her face smacked against the bloody floor, but her palms absorbed most of the shock.

The cabin's front door opened. Erin lifted her head and listened as she pictured Sam standing before a blood-soaked living room. There hadn't been an inch of living space in the small cabin that Erin hadn't bled on. Gummous brown viscera coated the floors.

"Christ," Sam said from the front room.

Sticky footsteps crossed the cabin and drew closer to the bathroom. Erin pushed herself from the floor. Pasty blood contaminated her freshly washed body. It clung to her face and arms, clots tangled in her hair.

"Erin?" He neared the doorway.

"I'm in the bathroom." Erin trembled. Her teeth chattered and she was unsure if it was because Sam was there or if she was about to collapse from weakness.

Sam appeared with a hand over his mouth and nose. "Jesus, Erin, what the fuck?"

"Help me?" She didn't expect the words to come out of her mouth. She didn't want his help, nor did she want anything to do with him. But she *needed* help from someone. Anyone.

"Why did you come here? Why aren't you in the hospital?" His eyes were furious.

"I tried calling you. I didn't know where to go." Erin's

voice cracked.

Sam looked toward the floor at Erin's feet. A steady ruby flow seeped down her legs, between tiles. It oozed toward the doorway, toward Sam.

Sam backed up, lip curled in disgust. "This needs to be over between us."

Uterus contracting, Erin hunched over with a sharp stabbing pain in her vagina. She reached between her legs. Another massive clot passed and fell to her hand. Black-red membrane and agglutinated blood seeped between her fingers.

"You did this to me." Her chin quivered. Tears burned her eyes and streaked down her cheeks.

Sam took another step back. "What are you talking about?"

"This started when you made me…" She couldn't find the strength to say the words.

His eyes narrowed. "I didn't *make* you do anything."

"You… *made*… me." Her words came out in a whisper, but with fierce conviction.

Sam pulled a foot free from the tacky floor and gave it a shake. "Get out, Erin. Get help."

Tremoring hands lost control to her rage. She launched the massive blood clot at his chest. It smacked against a pale blue polo shirt and adhered.

Sam danced in a panic, shaking his shirt like a snake had landed on his chest.

"How's that feel?" Erin screamed. She reached between her thighs and scooped handfuls, catapulting them toward Sam.

Sam screamed and turned to run, but slipped in the small square hall. An overcorrection threw him off. He twisted, catching himself with a grip on the door frame to the basement. Sam stumbled backward and took a step down to gain footing on the steps.

But the steps were gone. Sam plunged into the lagoon of necrotic menstrual blood. Backside under, his hands and feet stuck above the surface as he sank.

Before Erin could tell him to hold still, Sam pulled his feet underneath.

"Sam, no! Don't move!"

Wide eyes, he looked to her with desperation, with disgust. His gag-reflex kicked in and he choked back vomit.

"You have to hold still."

"My foot is stuck!" Sam thrashed.

Erin leaned over the pool to extend a hand, but she knew he was too far away to reach.

His arms went under.

She extended fingers as far as they could stretch.

Sam twisted, head bobbing back and forth until he was up to his ears.

Erin ran for the mop in the bathroom. She rushed back and held it out over the pool, but he was gone.

She poked the mop handle into the pit and stabbed around for Sam. She poked through masses of stiff blood amidst pockets of more viscous fluid. She was unsure if the mop handle was even reaching him.

"Sam!"

A gentle ripple crossed the surface. She pictured

him underneath, struggling to pull himself to the top, only to be sucked deeper into the quagmire. His mouth filling with rotting clots of blood, packing his esophagus and blocking his airway. Choking to death on menstrual clumps.

The blood ripple ceased and a thick murky bubble popped to the surface.

Erin didn't give up on jabbing the mop deep into the pit hoping that he'd find it and grab on. But fatigue won. Her body surrendered. Erin sat back on her knees, and after a few minutes of staring into the basement, she climbed to a standing position. The trickling sound of steady drips splashed between her feet. The heavy drainage slowed. Worried about another clot, she reached down low to free it, but there was nothing blocking the flow.

Her vision tunneled. Erin rushed to the shower and sat with her back against the wall, letting the water cool her feverish state. Tears rinsed away in the downpour. She worried about being blamed for Sam's death. She worried nobody would believe her, or that she'd be labeled a whore for sleeping with a married man. She worried about going back to the hospital and inconveniencing the staff with her problems.

And she was tired of worrying.

Pink water swirled the drain. She shifted her pelvis, breaking free another small chunk of tissue. Once the lightheadedness stopped, Erin stood up to wash herself with shampoo before her trip back to the hospital.

She'd report what Sam had done, and what her parents had done years before. She'd take the heat of the world's judgment if it meant there was even a small hope to live without constant pain and suffering—or at least to prevent it from happening to someone else.

Eyes closed, Erin rinsed more shampoo from her hair and let the suds break apart the crusted blood on her legs.

When she opened her eyes, the water at her feet had turned clear.

And it stayed that way.

TANGERINE SKY

The memory of a tangerine sky lived rent-free in Sylvia Ramsey's head, and she needed to let it go. Her therapist had suggested releasing the image by painting it, so now a blank canvas stood between Sylvia and her mental health. Painting as a hobby vanished into the past because she feared her reds and yellows would accidentally mix on the palette, dredging up the color orange and the haunting image from sixteen years ago.

Arms hanging limp by her sides, Sylvia stared into the stretched canvas, attempting to imagine that sky, but her stomach churned as if she'd ingested a bucketful of cadmium orange acrylics.

For too many years, this color tormented her. It was time to reclaim it.

Sylvia closed her eyes. The 20 by 16-inch canvas burned into her retinas, displayed on the back of her eyelids. A rectangle of possibilities.

Could she paint those tangerine skies, dappled with fiery clouds as the sun dipped into the horizon? The black pier had cut across the water, speckled with tiny people. A little girl, twelve years old, spinning in the foreground as a silhouette, forever trapped against that hideous orange prison.

Sylvia opened her eyes. The memory of her little sister came to life as a phantom upon canvas. She should paint it. She *needed* to paint it. To reclaim the color. To memorialize her sister in the last moment she was ever seen.

It was the moment that forced Sylvia to grow up. She had only been fifteen, but if she were watching her sister more closely, Hanna would still be with her.

Another silhouette crept into the depiction in her mind. He took Hanna in his grip and stole her. Hanna's ponytail whipped to the side, but she left without a fight. She was so far away. Sylvia couldn't run fast enough against the tide of boardwalk strollers and bicyclists. The tangerine sky devoured Hanna's small silhouette forever.

After Hanna was taken, that hideous, monstrosity of a color in the sky appeared everywhere. During questioning, an officer peeled a mandarin at his desk nearby. Her eyes gravitated to the color of the fruit against the white cinderblock wall as his nubby fingers dug into the peel. That day, she'd hated the officer who casually thought of food during her tragedy. His sticky fingers were wet with blood-orange injustice, clinging to idle hands.

Sylvia gave up oranges. And carrots. She rejected every orange thing. The pumpkin-toned walls of her family kitchen suffocated her so many times, her parents had to repaint them blue. She avoided orange like it was a monster that could swallow up everything she loved.

Not that she allowed herself to love anything any-more.

Her job came first. The rage which fueled her was all there was to live for. After school, she'd studied criminal justice and then became a police officer, doing grunt work for years until she made detective. That's all she'd ever wanted since August 18, sixteen years ago—to do what the sticky, mandarin-eating man never accomplished. Sylvia would bring down child trafficking rings. She'd hunt them and scour those stains from humanity. In some small way, she'd always hoped to find her sister, but she'd come to terms with the reality years ago.

Painting could aid with processing those imprisoned emotions. Spew the bottled anger.

A knock at her door broke her focus from the canvas.

Her chest tightened, breath trapped beneath the weight of revelation.

Go away.

Another series of knocks thundered through her veins.

"Yo! Ramsey!" Martinez called through the door.

The pulse between her ears beat in sync with her footsteps as she approached. She unlocked the deadbolt and opened the door a crack. "What?"

He scowled. "What do you mean 'what?' Why aren't you at the bar celebrating? We've been calling you all night."

"I know…"

"Damn!" He covered his nose as the stench from her apartment hit him. "What the hell died in there?"

"It's best to breathe through your mouth." She stepped into the hallway and closed the door, feigning a smile. "The rat poison my super put down—they're dying in the walls. Add to that, I haven't been home much lately so everything in the fridge is…well, there's some Chinese in there that—!"

"Alright, alright… but are you good? You need to talk or whatever?"

She cringed. "I don't need to talk."

"I know this is a big one for you. You got the fuckers!" Martinez held up a fist and bit his lower lip. "This one meant a lot—your life's work, or whatever. I thought you'd be celebrating with us all. But after the raid, you were gone. I figured I'd stop in to make sure—"

"I'm fine!" Sylvia rolled her eyes. "Look…" She held up her hand, fingers still wrapped around the handle of a paintbrush. "I thought I'd be celebrating this moment too. But I just need some quiet for a minute. I need to process." She waved the brush. "Therapist's orders. You feel me?"

Martinez nodded and placed a hand on her shoulder. "Yeah, okay, but—"

"But what? You wanna talk feelings? Come in and help me bust open some walls looking for dead rats? Have some Chinese? I think there's some hairy lo mein in one of those boxes…"

"You're nasty." He pointed a finger at her face. "But we love you anyway. Okay, Ramsey. You do what you gotta do tonight—tomorrow, though—you, me, and Burke are getting drinks!"

"Okay."

"Promise?"

"Get the fuck out, Martinez." She smiled.

After Martinez left through the elevator, Sylvia re-entered the apartment. The odor assaulted her senses on reentry.

Standing in the dining area which she converted to an art studio, Sylvia faced the small kitchenette. On the floor where she'd left him, wrapped in a blue tarp, lay the body of Victor Cambridge. She pulled back a corner of the tarp to expose his face—pale, eyes open, slack jaw. The acrid odor of death plumed. She turned away, holding her breath.

He was a young guy, maybe in his late twenties. Peeling back the tarp further revealed thin shoulders and the rest of his shirtless torso. Congealed blood had pooled in his gaping abdominal cavity.

Immediately after the raid, Sylvia didn't feel the much-anticipated relief she'd been expecting after all these years. Her team took down an entire syndicate of child traffickers in one sweep. They got the head of the organization in hand cuffs, but as he was carefully guided into the backseat of a cruiser, a sorrow filled Sylvia's heart. Sorrow that it wasn't the man who took her sister. There were others, just like this dead guy on her kitchen floor, who acted as lures. Every foul piece of shit who ever stole a child was still out there. The tangerine sunset bled out of her brain and into her heart, filling it with rage. It pumped into her veins, pulsing through her entire body, feeding every organ and every muscle until she was so full of fury she wanted to cut it out of herself.

The orange rage had propelled her to the last known residence of one of the men. Victor wasn't in the building during the raid, and he was too low on the totem pole to go after without risking the big-picture win. All guns needed to be on the main location, but as soon as it was complete, she needed to get Victor too.

She needed all of them. Every last one wiped away, blank like the canvas.

The moment was a blur—a splotchy nightmare. Without telling anyone where she was heading, she had apprehended Victor at home. The scrawny guy was in his underwear, scratching his head as he opened the door. After tackling him to the cement floor of his apartment, the memory went hazy. He pulled a knife from somewhere and she fought it from him. During the tussle, she must have slashed into his belly. Glimpses of a memory flashed in her mind—the knife repeatedly sank into his gut. Gouging, carving until her arms tired. His desperate eyes pleaded with her to stop, but she couldn't.

Tangerine skies were blotted out completely by the fiery clouds in her head. As she spewed the madness from her body, the clouds rained red until she couldn't see the traces of orange any longer.

In a daze, she had stuffed him in an oversized rolling duffle and lugged him to her vehicle.

Now, he lay covered by a tarp in the kitchen, decomposing until she could process how she'd gotten here. Dreams of violence and righteous vengeance had come to her in the past, but she never thought they'd ever manifest as more than wishful thinking.

She stared at the canvas, desperately seeking guidance.

Sylvia grabbed a large tube of acrylic lemon yellow and pressed it directly to the canvas, squeezing a small splotch onto the surface where a sun would soon be painted.

"A sunset…" she whispered. "Release it."

She smeared the streak of paint with a brush, pressing it into the white backdrop.

Her peripheral vision couldn't ignore the blue tarp in her kitchen. Toes poking out of the end. Eyes brimming with tears, she turned to face him. He'd taken so much from her… from others.

She launched toward him, swinging her foot into his ribs. Bones snapped under the assault. She kicked again and again until his ribs collapsed. In her fury, she'd squeezed her tube of paint so hard that the lemon yellow seeped out and landed onto his body—a ropey yellow glob atop his bloody insides. Mangled intestines and clotted blood beneath.

The fiery red insides bled through the yellow. Sylvia's fist remained clenched, squeezing out long ropes of paint which fell into his body cavity. Tears dripped into his open abdomen, mixing with paint and bile and organ and blood.

She admired the colors, yellow and red… how she loved them on their own. Knees buckled and she dropped, arms held high above her head with the paintbrush in hand, she plunged it into his gut, stabbing, screaming, hoping the anger might take away the pain. But all she got was a mixture of yellow and the blood of a monster, swirling into the perfect shade of orange. She stirred, hypnotized by the dance of colors, the fluidity of movement, and the catharsis of justice.

With her palette restored, she smeared the paint-blood mix onto the canvas. Varying shades from blood-red orange to bright yellow. A fading skyscape of color recreated a replica of the backdrop which devoured her sister.

The hours ticked by and Sylvia Ramsey finished her painting. She sat in the corner, body smeared with yellows, black, red… and orange. It clung to her clothes, her fingers. The image lived outside of her mind. On the canvas, a silhouette of a spinning girl, forever joyful in that moment before the terrible thing. Forever dancing against a tangerine sky.

HERE FOR YOU

The day my daughter was born was the day I began to disappear. Literally.

I thought my vision was failing as I stood before a foggy bathroom mirror on the first day home from the hospital. Swiping my hand across the surface did nothing because it wasn't coated in a layer of condensation. No matter how hard I wiped, how much glass cleaner was sprayed, my image in the mirror wouldn't clarify.

Every mirror was the same—slightly out of focus. Then, one afternoon, a neighbor stopped by to congratulate me and see the baby. She stood in the foyer beside me, ogling over Amy in the baby carrier. The mirror in the hall reflected us both. My neighbor's image was normal, while I remained unfocused.

There was nothing actually wrong with my face, though. The neighbor said, "I looked fine," and "Amy looks just like you." Fortunately, the rest of the world, including Amy, was in focus.

Doctors sent me to ophthalmologists… and then back

to more doctors. Seeking psychological help landed me in counseling sessions—more sessions than I could count. We talked about when Dave left me. We talked about the stress of motherhood. We talked about all the things that could've led me to this point. Hours and hours in a room with someone who made it clear that it was all in my head. The therapist robbed too much time away from my daughter. And since there was technically nothing wrong with me, I stopped seeking answers and accepted my condition—one of motherhood's many tolls, I guess.

As Amy grew, she came into focus while the blurring of my features worsened. Photographs of myself appeared to lose sharpness. Memories of my life before being a mom became indistinguishable smudges on those photos. None of that mattered though, because Amy got sick.

Hodgkin's sent her in and out of the hospital for two years. I cut my work hours to be with her, and in turn, I lost the promotion. I failed to maintain relationships with other people. Nobody mattered but Amy. Her health and happiness was the only thing that mattered.

But when she rang the bell at the hospital for the last time, my life didn't change much. Amy's hospital visits turned into after-school activities. They filled the calendar, and my time belonged to her. Sports, clubs, sleepovers, parties, heartbreaks… I gave all of myself so she could grow and thrive.

With every new pimple and inch grown, I blurred away. And with each feature fading, I lost focus of who I was inside as well. Who I used to be.

I would forever belong to Amy. And while there was no resentment toward my daughter, I sank further into a hole of despair every day. My blur became a void I couldn't escape, and so I stopped trying.

Her late teen years arrived, and I'd lost myself completely. I couldn't remember what I looked like before. Old picture albums revealed my daughter, friends, and family as clear as reality, but I was out of focus.

That's when the dark thoughts came. The endless test of my sanity drove me to wonder if I should end it all. Maybe I could cut myself so deep that some old part of me would bleed out. Maybe I'd feel something again. Some feeling that wasn't a mom's pride, or a mom's fear, a mom's anxiety, a mom's love… Maybe I'd feel some emotion that was mine alone.

But the blurry me whispered one word from the mirror: *selfish.*

I tried doctors and therapists when those dark, invasive thoughts became overwhelming, but when they suggested keeping me in a facility, away from my girl, I knew I had to suck it up a little longer.

Suicidal feelings lingered, but I tucked them away. Maybe one day, when Amy was old enough to be on her own, I could finally be free. Then, I could close my eyes and vanish completely.

Until that day, I needed to be there for my daughter.

So, I focused on everything else: work, the dust on the shelf, Amy's homework problems… and most clearly, Amy herself.

Especially today as she stood at the podium giving

the valedictorian speech. Amy's intelligence, her strength, confidence, kindness… her *face*… were more vivid, more hi-def than I'd ever seen myself.

With her journey reaching adulthood, I hoped my old self might return. I wished the face I once knew would reappear. But that woman is gone.

I stare into the mirror on this evening after Amy's graduation and see nothing looking back at me. My face is an empty skin canvas. No shape, no nose, mouth, or eyes. My trembling fingers explore the landscape, feeling curves and fine hairs; some palpable ghost of whom I used to be is there, but I'll never see her again.

It's time to free that ghost of this prison.

The cool edge of a box cutter is pressed gently against my wrist. I stand at the mirror, eyes stinging with tears. They fall in hot tracks along my cheeks. Their salty taste on my lips, proving some part of me is still there.

Though the blade has not yet dug into flesh, it may as well be jabbed into my core. I imagine it there, digging in, stirring around, and setting me free. I sob in agonizing pain, but all that is reflected is a blank oval where my face used to be.

"Mom?" A knock accompanies Amy's voice at the door.

I fight through the torment, catching my breath with a gasp. "Yeah, honey?"

"I don't know what goes on this part of the application."

I regain control over my quaking body. Teeth chatter. My shaking hand rests the blade on the edge of the sink and I look back to the blur in the mirror.

I've given everything of myself, raised her to be a strong individual. And yet, I can't bring myself to leave her. What do I possibly have left to offer her?

But there will always be new things in her life. New experiences she'll need to navigate. Applications. University. Jobs. Relationships, and eventually—maybe—parenthood. Amy still needs me. She will always need me in some way.

"Mom?"

I force a promise with my tremoring voice. "I'll be there in a minute."

I'll have to be there for all the minutes after, too. I stand before the indecipherable image in the mirror and whisper through gritted teeth, "I'll always be here."

LEGACY

Ma's soul was so evil that Father Vance forbade her from being buried in the church cemetery. Maeve and Ryan had to put their mother's remains in the ground behind the farm. It was as good a place as any, they supposed, but that's when the crops died. It started with the grass over her burial site. It shriveled into a brown patch like a dog had pissed all over her grave.

Ryan had taken a swig from a bottle of bourbon.

"Aren't you going to pour a little for Ma?" Maeve asked.

Ryan shook his head. "She had more than enough when she was alive." He spit to the side of her grave. "I wish I pissed on her grave myself."

It didn't take long before the death spread from the grass around Ma's burial site and across the field. Tall grasses withered and crumbled to dust. A day later, the great row of elm trees that bordered the property shed their leaves and their branches turned gray. The field of alfalfa was dead the morning after that.

"It's Ma," Ryan said. "She ruined everything she touched."

"She did not." Maeve—ever the defendant of Ma's actions—put her hands on her hips and stood up to her brother. "She was good to us."

"She was good to *you*."

"Don't start with that—"

"You were her *girl*. The girl she always wanted. She kept pushing out kids, hoping for a girl, but just got boys."

"Ryan, I'm warning you—"

"Then *you* arrived she didn't have to keep *accidentally* losing babies to crib death no more."

"I'm so sick of this rumor! You're here, ain't you? Why would she keep you?"

"I was her first…" Ryan fought the swell of heartbreak and anger in his chest. "*You* were her favorite.

"Can't we just let Ma rest in peace?" Maeve said.

"She don't deserve peace after what she done."

Everyone knew it, but nobody could prove it. There was a darkness to Ma that lurked at surface level, it was an eerie evil, unseen, but constantly leaving a mark on the world. Ryan knew all along that she didn't love him. Just like she didn't love his brothers that came after him. He couldn't remember them because he was only a baby, but he believed the stories he'd heard in town.

"That's not a nice thing to say," Maeve said.

Ma showed love to nobody but her precious Maeve, and even that relationship was toxic. Ma spent years grooming Maeve to be a mini-version of herself. As Maeve got older, she'd included her on her get-rich-quick schemes, which always ended badly.

But Maeve was kind. Maeve had a heart that Ma couldn't touch. Where Ma's eyes were black as her soul, Maeve's were a coppery brown—like an innocent doe. Ryan believed Maeve to be too good of a soul—untouchable, beyond Ma's metastatic reach.

After all the crops died, Ryan had Ma's body exhumed from the farm. She was incinerated and her ashes were placed in a small urn which Maeve now clung to with delicate hands.

"It's not right what you did." Her lower lip quivered. "You shoulda let her be."

"The whole farm was dying."

"You know damn well there's no way she had anything to do with that."

Ryan shook his head. "Maybe not, but I don't want her evil on my land no more."

"She wasn't *evil*…" Maeve shrunk. "She was just broken." Tears streamed down her cheeks as she stood overlooking a meadow of wildflowers. Maeve claimed Ma loved to visit this hill beyond the farm. But Ma didn't *love* anything but her booze, her evil secrets, and her precious Maeve.

Ryan's lip curled in disgust. "When people leave this earth—if they're lucky—they get to make a mark on the world. Ma didn't leave just a mark…she left *scars*."

His eyes stung from tears that wanted to form, but he stopped letting those tears fall long after he'd escaped her abusive reach. He looked to his sister, who clutched the urn to her chest, and then stared out over the beautiful field of yellow and white. "Ma doesn't deserve to be here. We should've left her ashes in the incinerator."

"How can you say that?" Maeve unscrewed the lid. The spring breeze whipped her hair across her face. "Ma, I'm so sorry you didn't have a chance to make things right."

That monster would never have tried. Ryan was drawn to the opening of the urn. Something inside longed to be released. Something powerful and wrong…it wanted out. Everything about the moment felt sacrilegious in some way.

"Wait…" Ryan held his hand up. "Put the lid back on."

A moment of panic set in Maeve's eyes before she reached inside the urn with a quick thrust. She flung her arm out, tossing ashes into the air. Gray ash billowed into a plume and caught on the wind, dispersing into the clear blue sky.

Ryan held a gasp.

"She deserves to be *here*," Maeve said. "No matter what she did. Everyone deserves a proper memorial."

"She deserves nothing beyond death and darkness."

The wind shifted.

The grass below Maeve's feet turned from green to yellow. The blades withered to tan and crunched underfoot. Maeve took a step back. Over the meadow, wildflowers went limp and gray as bits of Ma's ashes settled to the earth.

Maeve's hair no longer whipped across her face, but instead it blew straight behind her with the changing wind. Maeve's eyes were hopeful, watching Ma set free on the wind.

But the wind in Maeve's face carried with it remnant ash which hadn't yet settled to the earth. Maeve coughed, gagging on the dust of Ma's remains. She crumpled to the ground, clutching the urn to her chest. Veins swelled in her gnarled hands. Her neck tensed as dark vessels appeared beneath translucent skin.

Ryan knelt by her side, begging that his sister be all right, but before he could help her, she got back to her feet. Tears drooled from her clenched lids. She sucked in a deep breath and opened her eyes. Irises transformed from bright copper to midnight black.

Ryan's heart shattered as Maeve stared upon the desiccated meadow and grinned over the scars left behind.

FOURTEEN GALLONS

Sideways sunbeams pierced the fog over dewy grass and decomposing corpses. Evaporated bodily fluids ascended from the melted skin-bag bodies that peppered the neighborhood. Their insides had eviscerated into liquid. The fog swirled and levitated above the neighbor's body like a delicate ghost trying to escape, but reluctant to leave the only life it ever knew.

It reminded Meredia of steam from a hot cup of tea. If she closed her eyes, she could imagine the smell of an herbal blend. She could taste it on her lips. It was quiet enough to transport herself out of her home and to the beach, listen to the waves crash against the shore. Elle would sit by her side like they did when they were teens, slathering on sunblock as the sun rose higher, soaking in the salt life from sunrise to sunset. That was back before life became filled with other things to do. Back before they journeyed into adulthood which was supposed to be full of adventures galore. Their beach days became work days and before they had a chance to realize that they weren't living the lives they wanted, the world ended.

Last month as the stars disappeared behind a muddy haze, only a faint orange glow of the moon could shine through. In daylight, one could stare directly at the sun without squinting. Scientists from the ESA claimed remnant dust from the creation of the solar disk was to blame. A haze so thick, it blotted out all starlight. A nebula that had been floating unseen through space since the formation of the solar system billions of years ago. Others theorized the nebulous structure had regathered—bits and pieces of dust pulled together over time and encroached on Earth's orbit.

Whatever it was, when Earth blasted through the planet-sized cloud, bits of rock and ice crashed through the atmosphere and lit up the sky as meteors. The shooting stars burned so bright that they could be seen in daylight. In the evening, there were so many the darkened landscape lit up as if the world was on fire. And it rained starfire all day and night.

When the meteor storm was over, the muddy haze was gone and starlight pierced clear black skies once again. Everything went back to the way it was before. Everything seemed okay. Photographs and news stories faded into the background noise within a couple of days after the storm. Meredia and Elle returned to work and their adult-life routines…until a week later, when the first cases of sickness appeared.

Before the emergency messages became permanent on TV screens and devices, the news had warned about contaminated water supplies. Some microorganism brought to us by the dust cloud. When ingested, the water was like salt on a slug. It ravaged the human body, mutilating muscles and connective tissues. It turned tough skin and organs into a puddle of goo.

About a week ago, Meredia's neighbor had crawled from her house, elbows giving out beneath the weight of her body as her insides melted. A leathery shell deflated, skin clinging to bone as pureed insides oozed out of orifices. It reminded Meredia of a fast-food restaurant's pink slime meat—the same kind of meat Elle had refused to put in her body for years for the sake of the planet. Elle had always said that the excessive use of water and land for raising livestock—livestock that would be slaughtered and mashed into a patty of unidentifiable substances—had to be reduced. And Elle loved the planet enough to make the necessary changes. And Meredia loved Elle enough to give up meat three times a week.

She'd kill for a burger now. Or to sit outside on a beautiful spring day. If the outside couldn't kill her, today would be the kind of day she'd like to skip work and go to the beach. She wished she skipped work more often back then, before it all fell apart.

Fluffy cumulus clouds hung against an electric blue sky. Meredia imagined all that burning dust of the meteors being snatched up by the clouds. Tiny rain droplets collecting on the dust and then falling to the earth and ocean as rain. Bits of the universe crashing to the ground and making puddles full of tiny alien beings—puddles that her bare feet would never again get the chance to splash into.

"Why do kids stop splashing in puddles?" Meredia asked.

Elle's tired eyes raised from her lap to meet hers.

"It's still fun, splashing in puddles, so why do kids stop as they grow up?"

Elle's shaking hand brushed some hair from her forehead. She'd been wasting away faster than Meredia. Her metabolism was a beast, requiring an insane number of calories just to breathe and blink. Elle entertained the question. "I stopped because I liked wearing nice clothes."

Meredia tried to smile. Even smiling felt like a struggle for her muscles.

"Seems like a silly reason now, doesn't it?" Elle asked.

"I suppose so. Nice clothes don't matter so much."

"We got so caught up in doing all these important things…SAT prep, studying, volunteer hours, work-studies…" Elle huffed.

"None of it mattered."

"Beach cleanup? Water conservation? What good was saving the planet?" Elle said. "I guess it was all for nothing. Nothing to do now but suffer defeat." Elle licked her lips, dry and cracked from dehydration.

They ran out of bottled drinking water two weeks earlier. Since then, they'd rationed and sipped the fluid from canned beans and mixed veggies. Their food dwindled as quickly as the world's population.

Meredia and Elle sat at the kitchen table and watched the empty bird feeder outside as the morning sun rose above the neighbor's fence. There'd been no sign of a bird in weeks. Or a squirrel, or the neighbor's hound dog who used to bark incessantly. She'd love to hear that damn dog bark again. She'd love to see and hear a lot of things if she had the chance, but all the things she wanted involved being out there where it wasn't safe.

The world outside her doorstep had dew on the grass and a thick cloud of humidity. Microscopic killers floating in the breathable air. Windows and vents had been shut for weeks, stagnating the air inside their home. Potted plants went dry without watering, withered, and stopped producing oxygen. It was only a matter of time before Meredia and Elle succumbed to the fate everyone else had to suffer.

All those people out on their lawns, in a final and frantic escape from their homes for help that would never come. Melted insides returning to the soil.

"I read somewhere that the human body has 14 gallons of water inside," Elle said. "We just carry it around with us."

A weak smile twitched at the corner of Meredia's lips and her eyes grazed over Elle's gaunt frame. "Not anymore. We're so dehydrated, I think I'd be surprised to find an ounce of water inside of us."

"I guess the Earth is getting some of its water back as people die, huh?" Elle raised an eyebrow. "Take that, humans."

Meredia felt a hint of humor in her heart, but she couldn't laugh. Soon, they'd go into organ failure from starvation, and she figured they'd suffer a long and painful death. The thought of it haunted Meredia so much that she'd considered ending it all. The two of them could pop some pills—if they had anything stronger than Tylenol—and let the world dissolve away.

The thought of escape disappeared as the screech of tires on pavement cut through the silent neighborhood.

They leapt to their feet and ran to the picture window in the living room, craning their necks to see down either side of the street. They hadn't heard a vehicle—not even on the nearby highway—in days.

"I think it came from that way." Elle pointed to the east.

An engine grew louder and a car appeared with the sun chasing it. A glowing beacon of hope but also a harbinger of terror. Early on, there was looting. Most people weren't interested in robbing those who were still alive—just the houses of the dead. But a lot of confusion and mistakes were made when people were hungry and desperate for survival. Man could turn savage when faced with life-or-death situations. Meredia hoped they wouldn't become those terrible people who hurt others to survive, but survival instinct is a strong influence.

The blue Mustang convertible tore a hole through the sunlit fog. The sound of screaming followed.

"It's Dave!" Meredia said.

"Who?"

"Disco Dave!"

Dave stood from his seat, shirtless, fist pumping in the air while he screamed "wooooohooooo!"

The old man, Dave, lived around the corner, stuck in the '70s, always in bell-bottoms and listening to disco, he lived freely and did what he wanted all the time. Even if that meant mowing his front yard in his underwear. Elle had been jogging by one day and said Dave waved with a smile, donning a pair of tighty-whities, claiming, "If you're not gonna live now, then when?" His antics were the topic of many dinner-time conversations.

As the car whizzed by, Dave smiled, wind in his long hair. He turned to face their house and did a double take. The Mustang screeched to a halt.

"Oh no." Elle shut the curtains to the picture window and backed away. "He saw us."

Meredia peeked from behind the edge of the curtain as Disco Dave leapt from his car. He wore board shorts and his silver hair streamed behind him as he jogged across their yard. "He's coming to the door."

"Don't answer it," Elle said.

"He saw us."

Elle sat pressed against the front door as if her frail body was strong enough to act as a barricade.

Dave banged on the door so hard, Elle jumped away with a squeal.

Meredia's heart thumped between her ears. Perhaps Dave had news. He was their neighbor—the weird one—but a neighbor nonetheless. She had to at least talk to him. She whipped open the curtain to the window by the door.

Dave pressed his hands against the glass. His skin clung to his bones. Bags under his eyes more pronounced than ever. "Hi!" His voice was slightly muffled through the thick glass. "You don't got no water left, do you?"

Meredia shook her head. "We ran out."

Elle stood behind Meredia tugging on her shirt.

"Me too." Dave said. "I'm taking a drive to check some stores and houses. Maybe get a bit of a joy ride in, at last."

"It's not safe out there," Meredia said, but it felt ridiculous exclaiming the obvious.

Dave shrugged. "You ladies should come on out of there. It's fine. Everything's going to be fine." He said it with the cool, collected confidence of a sane man, someone who believed without a doubt that everything would be all right.

"Do you have news?" Elle said, leaning over Meredia's shoulder. "Is there an update?"

"Yeah, I have news…" Dave looked to the sky and held his arms out wide. "It's a weather update. Partly cloudy with a chance of a breeze." Dave's peace-sign pendant swung across his sparsely haired chest. A sputtering chuckle spit through his clenched teeth as tears formed in his eyes. "It's too beautiful out to stay inside, ladies."

"We're fine in here. Thank you for checking in." Meredia nodded. "Let us know if you find anything."

"Oh…I'm not coming back." Dave pressed his face against the window.

She jerked away.

His face smeared across the glass. "I said you should come outside!" His lips parted and he pressed his mouth to the window and blew hard, billowing out his cheeks and raspberrying hot breath onto the glass like a kid.

Elle covered her mouth and backed away. "What's

wrong with him?"

Dave's saliva clung to the window.

"He's contaminating the house," Elle said.

"It's already all over your house!" Dave twirled away from the window. "It's everywhere." He charged back at them. "Just get it over with and get out here!" Dave lifted a plastic chair from the porch and swung it at the window. It ricocheted off and fell to the ground. He banged again with his fist. And again.

Elle screamed. Shaking, she backed into the kitchen. "Meredia! What do we do?"

Meredia dove for the baseball bat in the corner and held it up so Dave could see it. "Get the fuck out of here!"

Dave's hand smashed against the glass and a crack formed. He admired it with a smile and took a few steps back with his hands up. "All I'm sayin' is it's a beautiful day."

Dave ran to the car, jumped in, and burned rubber tire marks into the pavement as he pealed away.

Elle rushed to the window donning rubber gloves and ripped a long strip of duct tape with her teeth. She covered the crack, then tore off another strip. And another. Covering the crack at least five times. "Is it going to get in here? I think that crack goes all the way through. Is it in here?"

"I don't know."

"What the hell was wrong with him? Was it the infection? Does it mess with your brain first?" Elle rapid-fired unanswerable questions. "Did he just lose his mind being alone? Is that going to be us? Are we going to lose our minds?" She buried her face in her hands. "Or are we going to just die of thirst?" She dragged her fingers down her red, puffy face, but no tears escaped Elle's eyes. Not enough fluid in her body for tears.

The sound of Dave's tires were long gone and the midday sun beat down on the house. No more than a can of kidney beans remained in the cabinet—from that time Elle tried to make chili. That was the only food they had other than the one special thing they'd been holding onto.

"Hey, you want to do something fun?" Meredia asked.

Elle shook her head. "I don't think that's possible anymore."

"We have to try, or we'll end up losing our minds like Dave. Let's eat the rest of it now." Meredia walked into the kitchen.

"I thought we were going to save the rest for our first anniversary."

"That's a month away. And we need the calories." She opened the microwave and pulled the Tupperware from inside. The top tier of their wedding cake had been in their freezer since last year. A couple of weeks ago when the power went out, they moved it to the microwave. They'd been picking at it for extra calories, and Meredia hoped that if they could make it last until their one-year anniversary next month, that maybe they'd survive this. That maybe they'd make it forever. Now, they weren't sure if they'd make it until tomorrow.

"Do this one thing for me," Meredia said. "It'll be fun."

She pulled their wedding dresses out of the storage

chest, and Elle and Meredia prepared for a final romantic dinner.

Meredia squeezed into the fitted lacy thing that fit better last year.

"This is silly…" Elle shook her head.

"Exactly the point." She broke off a bit of the cake with her fingers.

Elle did the same wearing her A-line white classic gown. They stood at the end of the table and fed each other a nibble of cake from their hands. After Elle took a bite of the stale cake, Meredia shoved the remaining piece into her face. Cake crumbled into dry clumps, frosting smooshed into her face and fell to the floor.

Elle jammed her piece back at Meredia in a moment reminiscent of their wedding day. As she pulled away laughing, squealing in a brief moment of delight, cake smeared across her neck. For the first time in weeks, they both laughed.

Meredia's eyes went to the floor, where there were crumbs and frosting at their feet.

"That was wasteful…" Elle's face turned serious in an instant. Laughter fell to regret.

Meredia hung her head, wiping cake from her face and neck with the curtain.

"What are you doing?" Elle laughed. "Those are nice curtains."

"All of our hand towels are gross."

"So you use the curtains? What's next? Wiping our bottoms with the bedsheets?" Elle's mouth was agape for a moment before she broke into hysterical laughter. She held her ribs and winced.

Meredia felt it too. An ache inside. Organs angry with the lack of nutrients. Muscles weak without protein and calories…without water. Now their stomachs churned with the stale chocolate cake. It was the first thing in their bellies since they shared half a can of chick peas the day before, slimy fluid and all.

They couldn't stomach anymore. Chocolate smears stained the front of their dresses. Dresses that were once kept in boxes to be preserved for some reason they couldn't explain. For what, their daughters? Some future life that would never come?

Elle's hair was twisted up in a clip. Messy fly-away strands stuck out in all directions. She held her stomach and cringed. "Cake was a bad idea."

"Probably…but it was fun."

The temperature soared and before long they were stripped out of their wedding dresses and lounging in their underwear. Sweat-soaked cotton clung to their skin.

"Any more fun ideas?" Elle asked fanning herself with the unpaid mortgage bill. "I need more laughing. Less existential dread."

"If things were normal, what would you want to do?"

"You mean, if I didn't have to go to work?"

"Yeah. Anything. Today is a regular day. The contamination never happened. And you don't have to work or save the planet. What do you want to do?"

Elle closed her eyes and inhaled through her nostrils. "Go to the beach. See the ocean again. Smell the salty air…"

The sight of her joy made Meredia want the same thing. They were beach rats as kids and even though they were only a twenty-minute drive from the shore, they rarely visited in their adult years after life got so busy with work and keeping up with the house.

Meredia leaned in, took Elle's hands, and smiled. Eyes stinging with the need to cry, her teeth chattered. "Let's go to the beach, Elle."

"What are you saying?"

Her lip quivered. "Let's go to the beach."

"You want to give up?" Elle's spine became rigid.

"It's not giving up."

"It's accepting our fate…It's walking into the fire!"

"It's—"

"I'm not going to kill myself!"

"No. We're not *killing* ourselves," Meredia said. "We're taking the last of what's left of our lives and—instead of withering away behind the walls of this mortgage we'll never pay—we're choosing to *live*."

"I want to live as long as we can."

Meredia backed against the wall. "I do, too." Wet skin clung to the cool surface. She pulled away quickly. It wasn't just her sweat clinging to the wall. Humidity had soaked through allowing condensation to form on the interior walls.

"Is that outside water that got in?" Elle asked. "Or is it moisture that's been cycling inside the house?"

The water on the walls dripped down. Meredia was thirsty enough that she wanted to lick it off, whether it had little alien organisms in it or not.

Elle hugged her arms around her waist. "Oh my God. We're not safe anywhere anymore, are we?"

"I don't think we ever were. It was only a matter of time, right?"

She nodded. "Is it going to hurt? It looks like it hurts." Her eyes darted to the window, to the neighbors lying in their yards, melting into unidentifiable puddles.

"I don't know. Dave didn't look like he was hurting. But if we wait to starve, or die of dehydration, I think it'll be so much worse."

Elle used the curtain to wipe the moisture from Meredia's back.

"Who knows? Maybe Dave was onto something. Maybe it's not in the air anymore. Maybe we can find some water on the shelves to hold us over for a few days. And then another few days… Maybe…"

"Yeah…Maybe…"

Meredia knew as well as Elle that neither of them believed in any of the maybes. But they had to hope for something.

Without an item packed, Meredia and Elle stood hand in hand before their front door in their undergarments.

"Are you ready for adventures galore?" Meredia asked.

Elle nodded. "It's about time."

The front door cracked open, peeling away from the swollen frame in the heat of the afternoon. Keys in hand, Meredia swung open the door and was met with thick humid air. The smell of death lingered in the neighborhood. The acrid aroma filled her nose, but the sound of the breeze rustling through the trees met her ears and she soaked in the experience.

"Here goes." She took a long deep inhale and felt free for the first time in weeks. Maybe the air was cleaner now, and they'd be free like Disco Dave, or maybe she'd just inhaled a lung-full of microorganisms that would start dissolving her from the inside out over the next few days.

They removed the top of the Jeep and settled into their seats. Meredia backed out of the driveway, pealing her tires as they screeched out of the neighborhood.

Wind in their hair, they drove to the shore.

A few dead bodies peppered the beach—souls with the same idea to enjoy their last moments taking in the beauty of their planet. The salty beach air sat in Meredia's nose and filled her body with delight.

"Earth will be fine, you know," Elle said.

Meredia scanned the bodies on the beach. Deflated skin-bags, liquid insides oozing into the sand and ocean.

Elle's lips twitched into a grin. "Maybe not us. Not people. We're done here. But our *planet*…she'll be fine." She leaned back on her elbows, soaking in the sun as waves crashed into the shore.

Meredia wondered how many other people were out there now, still alive, enjoying their final days. And how many were holed up in their homes, ready to shrivel away to nothingness in misery—holding on to some hope that there'd be more than just this miserable end.

More to life than becoming 14 gallons of water recycled back to the Earth.

THE HAUNTING OF SWAN LAKE

W hen I was a kid, I used to hide from my dad in the cellar of the Cooperstown Estate. It was a sprawling 10,000-foot home with multiple wings, so my sister Maria and I had plenty of space to play hide and seek. That's how I found the best hiding place in the entire house.

Dad's second-floor wing on the west end was off-limits, so I thought I'd be sneaky and hide up there, where Maria would never come looking for me. While I tiptoed down the hall, I could hear raised, muffled voices coming from a room with a thick oak door. Dad hadn't said much, but the other man inside went on and on about things I couldn't understand. That was the first time I'd ever heard Dad whistle that song. It was a classical tune—the same one that little Maria's pink ballerina music box played. I know it now as Tchaikovsky's Swan Lake. I used to listen to Maria practice it on her piano. A single key played for each note, and her small voice sang the letters:

a, b, c, d, e... c, e... c, e... a, c, a, f, c, a...

The notes of the song whistled from my father's lips, crudely, repetitively. Then, from outside the door, I heard a pop and the meaty thud of a man's body hitting the floor.

I ran, and Dad must've heard my footsteps because a door creaked open behind me as I sprinted around the corner.

"Danny boy!"

I didn't turn back. I hauled ass down the back stairs into the service kitchen and instead of blasting through the kitchen door on the main floor, I kept going down into the wine cellar. I'd hidden there before. In the far back of the cellar, past the last rack, where the lights couldn't reach beyond the necks of the wine bottles, there was a portion of the stone wall concealed in darkness. Back there, if I wedged myself behind, there was a small Danny-sized hole in the wall. An area where the wall was more wet clay than it was stone. Behind that wall, was a pocket in the earth no bigger than a small coat closet.

Dad opened the cellar door. "Danny? Come here, son. Let's talk about this…"

Heavy footsteps carried my hulking father down the steps. Each drop of his foot could've stopped my heart.

"I know you're down here."

I grabbed loose, palm-sized stones from the dirt floor and stacked them neatly, quietly.

And then Dad began to whistle the tune from Swan Lake, elongating the highest notes as he reached the basement floor. I couldn't see him at this point as I'd covered the hole in the wall from the inside. All I could do was hold my breath and hope he didn't find me there in the pitch black behind a pile of rock and clay.

He never did find me that day.

I crawled out hours later, hungry and shaking, wondering how hard he was going to whoop my ass. But the whooping never came. He looked at me in a different way after that. Like he was proud of me. I was the kid who didn't tattle on him, and because of that, he could mold me into a version of himself. A man I never wanted to be.

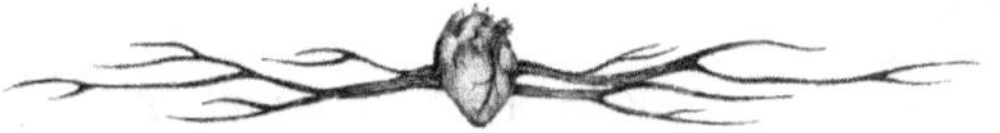

Now that I'm grown and he's out of my life for good, I stand in the doorway of his old office, recalling that day as a child when I ran from him, as well as a day only a month ago when I put a bullet through his head.

When Dad was missing in the morning, everyone thought he'd left, or that one of his enemies—he had plenty of them—nabbed him in the middle of the night. But only I know the truth. That monster attacked me, and in self-defense, I took him down. I did it for my family. I did it for Mom…for all the evil shit he'd done over the years…for what he made me do.

None of it matters much though, because Valerie and the kids are gone now. She took off with them farther upstate, said I wasn't myself and she needed a break. *A fucking break!*

And Mom is a hot mess. Investigators have been up her ass about Dad's whereabouts. They're close to having enough dirt on him to take us all down. So here I am again standing in his doorway as the moonlight filters through the window, unsure what the hell I'm doing here.

"Thank you for coming," Mom says.

She's close to sixty-years-old now and it's the first time I've ever looked at my mom and saw her as an old woman.

She sighs. "I already cleaned out his office and burned whatever I could find."

"Good…" I nod, hands on my hips. "So, you haven't heard from him?" I ask, knowing damn well nobody has heard from him.

She shakes her head, tears welling, but she fights them back. "Nothing. There's been no access to our bank accounts. I'm afraid he went and got himself—"

"Don't say that, Mom. We'll figure out what happened." I put a hand on her shoulder, but my attempt at consolation feels unnatural.

"I'm going to bed," she says. "We'll go through the rest of his things first thing in the morning."

My childhood bedroom is no more than a guest bedroom now, but there are too many bad memories to sleep here. Maria's room is just as bad. However, a few of her things still remain as a sort of shrine to the daughter Mom and Dad had given up on. After they cut her off and she left, they cleared out most of her things. Her antique dollhouse stands in the corner by a window, and her pink ballerina music box sits upon a doily on the dresser. There's a ghost of some sweet young girl in this room that never got to become anything more than a junkie. None of us have heard from her in nearly a year.

Tonight I choose to stay in Dad's old office—the one he turned into a bedroom during his final days. The place he took his last breath. I pull the gun out from the conceal-carry holster under my shirt—I don't go many places without it nowadays—and set it on the bedside table. It feels sinister kicking off my shoes and putting my feet up on his mattress, but I fucking earned this. I place my hands behind my head and lie back. A big *Fuck you* to Dad. He wanted me to take over his empire…so here I am.

I dream of the ballerina in the box and Swan Lake. She twirls like Maria used to, dancing to the steely, high-pitched tings pouring from the box. The tings morph into a different sound and Maria stops dancing. It's replaced by a new instrument—a slow whistle.

I run for my hiding place and duck behind the wine rack, but I'm too late. Dad is there, right where I buried his body last month. His face hasn't been crushed by my boot. It's still intact and inches from my own. His eyes bulge, capillaries burst and dribble small rivulets of blood. His expression snarls and saliva strings between lips while he grabs my arms. His mouth opens wide to scream, wider still, creating and impossibly large cavernous opening. But there's no screaming. All that escapes the gaping void is a melodic, slow whistle.

I snap awake with a gasp. The dream around me melts away, but Dad's face remains. Deep lines are etched into his skin, they lengthen and stretch as his mouth widens inches from my face. His hot breath reeks of death and rot. His pupils are dilated, nearly filling his irises with black sludge. I scrabble out of my bed, but his face follows.

No amount of swatting or blinking or shaking my head violently from side to side can make the image of him go away. He has no words or growls or any sound that makes sense. All that comes forth from his tunnel-like mouth is a pulsing, whistling tune.

I try to run but can't see anything but his fury, and I can't hear anything but that damned whistling. I crash into the wall and hear something break through the whistle.

"Danny!" Mom's voice cuts through.

I snap my attention toward her standing in the doorway.

"Are you okay?" She holds a hand over her heart, bracing herself by the frame.

Dad's face is gone. The whistle fades to no more than an echo in my mind.

"I'm fine…"

She stares, knowing damn well I'm not fine.

"Just a bad dream, Mom…sleepwalking, I think."

"I did't know you sleepwalk."

I rub my temples. "I guess I do now."

"Come eat something for breakfast and we'll talk."

"Yeah, okay, Mom."

That fucking face haunts me. It was Dad's expression right before he tried to shoot me last month as we struggled for control of his gun. The waking dream makes me want to puke and I can't even think about having breakfast. So, first, I shower, trying to wash away the image of his wrath. Lingering in the back of my mind is that tune, though. It plays on repeat like an earworm I can't quit. Five notes, climbing steadily higher, and then dropping, pulsing…

As I head downstairs to meet Mom in the kitchen, I can hear her whistling it now, too.

She's at the stove, scrambling eggs in a pan.

"Mom, can you not?"

She turns to face me. "You don't want eggs?"

"The whistling…that song—"

"Oh…" Her eyebrows knit together. "I didn't even realize I was whistling."

"I hate that song."

"What song?"

"You were whistling Swan Lake."

"Do I know that one? How's that go?" Mom scrapes the bottom of the frying pan with the spatula and smiles.

"Never mind…"

"I don't remember the last time I made you breakfast. This is nice."

I sit at the counter and rub my ringing ears. Somewhere deep within my head, that stupid song lingers, and when I close my eyes, his face is burned into the backs of my eyelids.

"How about you go downstairs and grab me a bottle of cab?" Mom says, putting two slices of bread in the toaster.

I head to the cellar door and open it. I haven't been down here since last month and revisiting feels stupid. *Fuck it.* I flick the light switch on and head down. As I reach the bottom, I can hear Mom whistling again. "Mom! You're doing it again!"

A muffled *What'd you say?* comes from upstairs,

nearly inaudible.

Before I can reply, the whistle no longer sounds like it's coming from upstairs. It's louder. Coming from somewhere in the cellar. Rising notes, *a, b, c, d, e... c, e... c, e...* in a sluggish, drunken whistle. A song he stole from my little sister, raping my memory of her of its innocence.

My eyes are drawn across the rows of wine racks toward the dark patch of wall in the back.

He knows I'm here. I can feel it.

The notes repeat: *a, b, c, d, e... c, e... c, e...*

I cover my ears to prove to myself that it's nothing more than a little musical tinnitus. Some psychologically fucked up thing going on in my head, but when I plug my ears, I can't hear it any longer. I lift my hands from the sides of my head and the sound returns.

We're not out of cabernet, are we? Mom's distant voice calls from upstairs.

I head to the third row where she keeps the cabernet and grab the first bottle I see. While I'm here, the volume of the whistling increases. Two rows away, behind the last rack, behind the soft clay, he's there.

What if he never died? Even after I smashed his skull with my boot, what if he somehow survived? I picture him back there, tucked in that little closet-sized hole in the clay and stone wall, trapped, unable to breathe, whistling Swan Lake in hopes someone will come rescue him.

The song crescendos as I stand only a foot from his burial site. The only place I knew his body would remain concealed. It was the perfect hiding place...until his whistle permeated the wall.

"Danny!" Mom calls, and I stagger away. With a bottle of red in hand, I sprint up the steps back into the kitchen but she's already gone.

"Danny?!" her voice calls from the foyer.

I leave the bottle on the counter and run to her, hand at my back, ready to pull my weapon. But when I get to the foyer, the police are already inside.

Dad continues to whistle and my heart becomes a lump of tissue I could choke upon.

They have a warrant, they say, and a woman directs the officers to different portions of the house. Half head upstairs, the others down the east wing.

The lead investigator, Marjorie Mann—Mom had already told me all about her—directs Mom and I back into the kitchen so Mom can shut off the stove. She has nothing on Mom or me, so she has us sit at the counter under supervision while her officers flip the place upside down.

Swan Lake grows so loud I worry someone will hear it. I look to Mom. Her eyes are panicked—telling me something without using words, but I can't know for sure what she's trying to communicate. I have to assume I'm not the only one who hears Dad's whistling. They'll find him down there if he doesn't shut up already. I try to make conversation, raising my voice above Mom's, above the investigator as she barks orders.

"Will you shut up?!" she yells, but I'm unsure if she means me, or the whistling.

What if they hear him? What if they find him dead in that hole downstairs? Or worse…alive?

Then I'll be the one going to prison…

a, b, c, d, e... c, e... c, e...

My eyes travel to the basement door, then back to Mom. She chews her lip and pours a glass of wine with a nod. She's trying to tell me something. I know for certain now. She's trying to tell me to go back to the wine cellar.

To cover my tracks. To shut him up

The song travels up the steps and through the door. It's loud enough now that the investigator will surely hear it.

As her back is turned, I sneak away from the counter and hurry to the basement door.

I run downstairs and sprint to the back wall, squeezing behind the last row of wine.

Where'd your son go? A muffled voice says from upstairs, but it's drowning in the repetitive melody of that damn song. *a, b, c, d, e... c, e... c, e...*

I dig. Fingernails gather clay and mud as I pull wet rock and earth away from the wall. Footsteps upstairs stomp about, but I am focused on getting to Dad and making sure they don't find him.

As the wall breaks away, the crescendo builds to a deafening volume. It pierces my ears.

A plume of putrefied fumes spills out of the hole in the wall, and I climb inside. My phone's light casts a blue glow on a body wrapped in a thick plastic sheet. There is no longer a face beneath. The necrotic and decomposing viscera of what used to be his face should not be capable of whistling, yet he does. The tune oozes out of liquefying flesh. I cover where his mouth should be with my hand. It sinks into the plastic. What used to be Dad's head collapses under my weight, and my hand submerges deep into his face.

And yet Dad continues to whistle.

The cellar door opens and footsteps clamor downstairs.

"Shut up!" I whisper to Dad, piling the stones back into place over the hole in the wall. I close us inside, packing clay against the backside of stone to keep light—and sound—from escaping. But it's no use. Dad only whistles louder.

I pull my gun from under my shirt and point it at him. "Shut up!" I snarl through gritted teeth.

The notes continue on a loop *a, b, c, d, e... c, e... c, e...* I hold the pistol to what's left of Dad's head and I pull the trigger. In this enclosed space, the gunshot sends vibrations screaming against my eardrums. On this new shrieking, ringing in my ears, Dad's whistling tune dances along a pulsing wave. Blood flow to my head throbs, creating a symphony of sounds, ever louder and louder…

It lures the police closer to the hidden space. *a, b, c, d, e... c, e... c, e...*

The Swan Lake music box ballerina dances to the song. Even she knows there's only one way to shut him up. Only one way to keep him from ruining everything for all of us. I press the barrel of the pistol against my own ear. Only one way that I can ensure to never hear him whistle that tune ever again…

…and I squeeze the trigger.

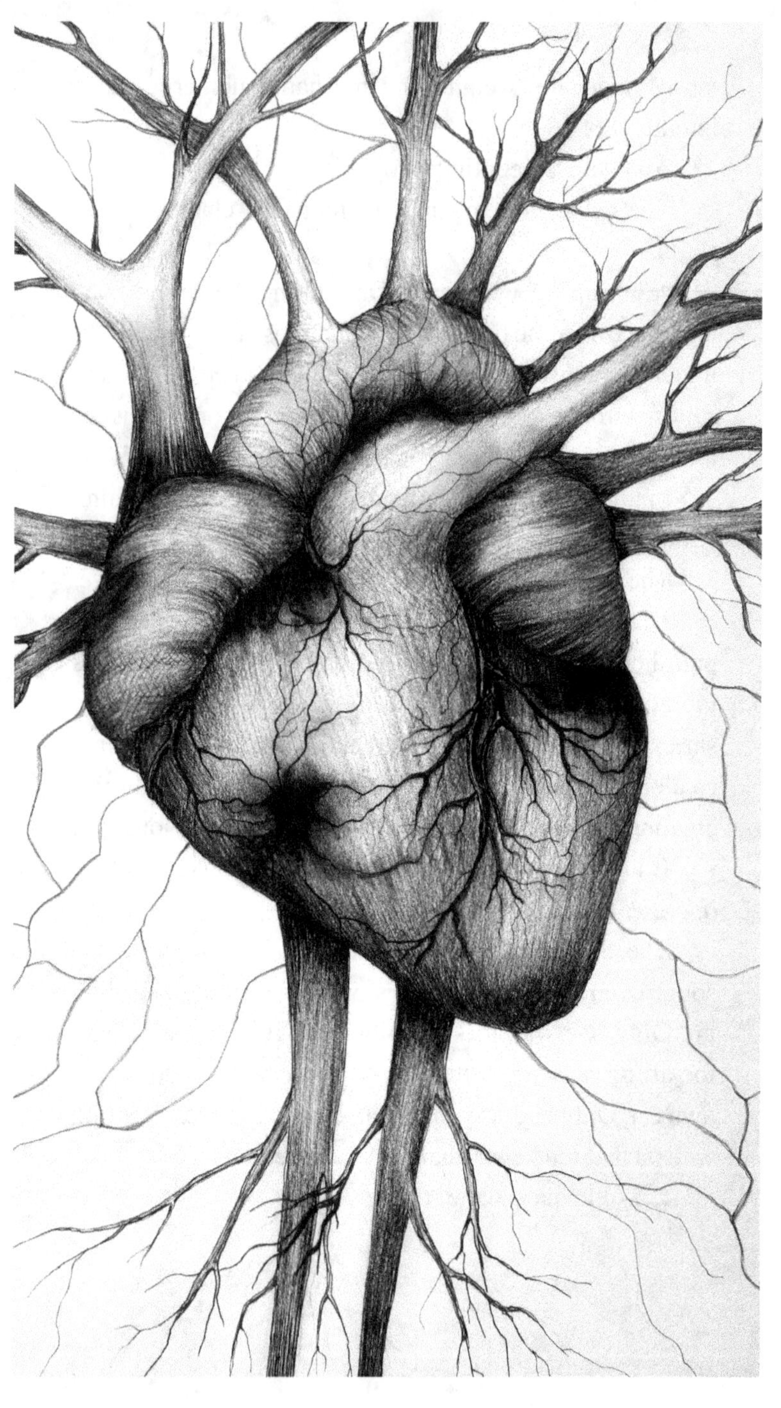

ABOUT THE AUTHOR

Red Lagoe grew up on 80s horror and carried her paranoia of slashers and sewer creatures into adulthood.

She is the author of the forthcoming novella, *In Excess of Dark,* from DarkLit Press (2024), as well as *Bloodstains by Gaslight* from Brigids Gate Press (2024).

Red has two more published collections, *Lucid Screams* and *Dismal Dreams,* and she is the editor of *Nightmare Sky: Stories of Astronomical Horror.* As a staff writer, she worked on Crystal Lake Publishing's *Still Water Bay* series, and her stories have been published in several anthologies and publications.

Amateur astronomy is her first love, so Red can often be found lingering in the inky shadows, among the beasts of the night, for a better view of the stars.

Find out more at www.RedLagoe.com.

AUTHOR'S STORY NOTES
(spoilers!)

Impulses of a Necrotic Heart

The theme of this collection came together because of this title. I had drawn a human heart that I was rather fond of—as seen on the cover—and it was the first time in my life that a title came to me before the story. I knew *Impulses* would be my titular story, but I had no idea what it'd be about. What impulses are necrotic in nature? I knew I wanted to explore the dynamics of the parent-child relationship. It comes up often in my work. So, I wrote about a man who—no matter how much he tried to fight it—couldn't escape the generational infection that came from his father's rotten core.

Hollowed Hearts

Yes, it's supposed to be *hollowed*, not *hallowed*. That's intentional. Wesley's heart is never full. His mother, while trying her best to take care of him as many single working moms do, fails to provide the one thing he craves the most, attention. His heart is empty, and he longs to soar like the birds…and like the bats. This story was written for *Lunatic Lullabies*, an anthology by Pyke Publishing to which I was invited to submit. It was a last-minute invite, and I wasn't sure what to do, so I dove into my own heart and dug out a little nugget of guilt from real-life experience. Those moments when I'm exhausted after a full day, and my son wants to play a game…and I sometimes say, "maybe tomorrow." From this guilty little feeling, I wrote *Hollowed Hearts*.

Don't Make It Weird

I wrote this for the Cursed Morsels Press open call for their sports and fitness body horror anthology, *Shredded*, and I was thrilled it was accepted. This was a massive rewrite and re-imagining of a non-horror flash piece I wrote years ago called *Developing on the Line of Scrimmage*. The story takes a real-life experience of mine from the mid-90s and turns it into a horror story. As a young teenager, I used to play pick-up games of football with the boys, and I was really good at it. But every time I stepped on the field, I got eye-rolls, and the boys who didn't know me rarely let me touch the ball. One day, I was killing it though. Intercepting passes, running for touchdowns, tackling… Then one of the tackles knocked the wind out of me. They huddled around me and started arguing that a girl shouldn't be playing. I dusted off my knees and was ready to get back on the line of scrimmage, but they stopped passing me the ball. I had a lot of bottled rage back then, and I would've loved to unleash on the field. But since I don't have gnarly creatures living in my tits, I guess I had to bring them to life on the page.

Consumer Alert

Consumer Alert has never been published, but it did place in the Dark Regions Press contest for the *Black Labyrinth: Possessions* anthology, which was never released. I've been holding onto this piece for years beyond the contract, and I finally decided to breathe some new life into it, and set it free. The theme was possession, so I made a woman become possessed over her possessions. Clever, *(eye-roll)* I know. But I think I pulled it off. How gratifying it is to *click, click, consume,* and have packages at our door within the week. How many times do we order something and forget, and then get excited when the mystery package arrives at the door? Meredith simply wanted to fill the void in her heart with anything she could get her hands on. There's a little Meredith in all of us.

Infectious Glow

I am a sucker for astronomy and love an opportunity to put some space and telescopes in a story. I'm also a huge zombie fan. So when Sinister Smile Press invited me to write a story for their anthology *If I Die Before I Wake: Tales of the Otherworldly and Undead*, I was down. Otherworldly and Undead translated to me as space and zombies, and I couldn't resist incorporating both. In late 2019, early 2020, the star Betelgeuse experienced unusual dimming. There was a lot of buzz in the amateur astronomy community, and while most scientists agreed it probably wasn't about to go supernova in our lifetime, we all couldn't help but wish it would! So with that excitement over potentially witnessing a supernova within our own galaxy, I created Chuck—a lonely, grieving astronomer with a heart problem during an apocalypse caused by Betelgeuse going supernova.

Arachnu

I have arachnophobia. Like, *legit* arachnophobia. Like, Jeff Daniels in the 90s movie *Arachnophobia,* arachnophobia. It's so bad, I feel fear and disgust and little tingly legs crawling up my spine just by looking at pictures of spiders. I've had terrifying encounters with them in my home. And while I can deal with it most days, there are times when the fear controls everything and I either freeze or thrash. Bugs may startle me and creep me out, so do rats and snakes…but I'm not *afraid* of those creatures. There's something about the stalking nature of spiders that sets me on edge. The brass-balls brazenness of the little fuckers to sneak up and crawl on a person. Who does that?? Spiders do. *Shiver.* So please, appreciate the pain and suffering I went through to write this story. It first appeared along with three more of my stories in a hybrid anthology collection by Cemetery Gates Media called *Seasons of Severance.*

The Glass Labyrinth

This was originally a 900-word flash fiction piece that I wrote for a contest. It didn't win—rightfully so. It was so bare-bones, it lacked depth and heart. But with two-thousand additional words and a breath of salty fresh air, it came to life. As a resident of a touristy coastal city, I've walked the empty boardwalk in the winter, and window-shopped locked stores and attractions. I've explored the glass maze here in town, and it was a hauntingly beautiful labyrinth. Since I can't help but ask, "What if…" when I'm exploring new places, the question came to me while bumping into another panel of glass: what if someone was trapped in the maze and never got out?

Dogwood

Yikes. I got a little dark with this one. Sorry, y'all. This was the "spring" story of the four stories I'd written for *Seasons of Severance*. When I think of spring, I think of the ephemeral beauty of the dogwood tree. I think of my childhood, running out to the tree over the hill, breaking off branches and placing them in a vase for my mom. They'd die only days later. *Dogwood* was born not only from this memory, but also from a drawing I'd done of a ghost (the drawing is not included in this collection). It was a sheet ghost, but instead of fabric, it was the heavy plastic in which the person had suffocated to death. It was a dark, twisted little idea that I combined with my spring story involving the dogwood tree and the innocence of childhood. Let's not cry anymore and move on…

Sensory Deprivation

Another story from the *Seasons of Severance* collection, *Sensory Deprivation,* jumps into the mind of a serial killer. I don't always care to write from the point of view of an undeniably evil person, because it's a tricky thing to do without glorifying the crimes committed. It was an uncomfortable POV to write from, but quite satisfying to make him lose his mind, self-mutilate, and get what was coming.

Blood Bogged

Worst. Period. Ever. The most blood I've ever written. Buckets of blood weren't enough…I needed a Biblical-level flow. *Blood Bogged* appeared in the Sci-Fi & Scary charity body horror anthology *Twisted Anatomy*. Was it a gag-worthy level of grotesquerie? Sure… but every ounce of period blood spilled was necessary to the story. And you can fight me on that. Erin had been taken advantage of. She was manipulated into sex by a man with more power than her, and it broke her. No amount of bleeding could purge the trauma her professor had caused, and it wouldn't stop until she stopped blaming herself. Also, the idea of clotted blood stalactites brings a sinister little grin to my face.

Tangerine Sky

First appearing in *Chromophobia*, an anthology exploring color, *Tangerine Sky* is a story about the color orange. This little tale began as a glimpse of a woman stirring blood with yellow paint to make orange. And that image became the body cavity of a dead man. And I couldn't have a character stirring paints in body cavities without a killer backstory. One that totally made it okay to kill a man, cut him open, and mix a new palette in his guts. And thus, *Tangerine Sky* was born.

Here For You

When I became a mother, I immediately became a different person. All of my time, everything I did, was for my kids. As the years went by, I felt as though I was growing further away from my former self, so far that I couldn't even recognize who I was anymore. For years, I felt as though I was no more than a mom. It's certainly how strangers viewed me, especially during that time when I was simply a stay-at-home parent. I had interests and aspirations but none of them were within reach. I had no regrets about becoming a mother, but it was a difficult feeling to navigate—feeling as though I existed solely to care for other people. Fortunately, I found my way back to myself. I found purpose outside of my family through creativity. Art and writing saved me from falling into depression. But there are a lot of people out there who suffer, never finding themselves again. *Here For You* explores, to an extreme, that terrifying feeling of losing track of yourself.

Legacy

By now, you're seeing that this parent-child dynamic sure does creep into my stories. *Legacy* was one of the winning stories for Cemetery Gates Media's monthly flash contest, themed "burial of the dead". It's in a similar vein as *Malignant Roots*, a flash piece in my collection *Lucid Screams*. In Legacy, we reach back into those themes exploring the inescapable darkness spread down through generations.

Fourteen Gallons

I wrote *Fourteen Gallons* for an open call submission which was accepted in the anthology *Midnight from Beyond the Stars*. I stayed on earth for this submission and made the focus of the story less about the alien life forms that caused an apocalypse, and more about one young couple at the end of the world. I am a sucker for an apocalyptic survival story, but I wanted a quieter, closed-door exploration of the fears that come with knowing you're about to die. The decisions that one must make in those final moments—to keep surviving, or to *live*? This one, like *Dogwood* and *Hollowed Hearts*, broke my heart to write.

The Haunting of Swan Lake

In my first short story collection, *Lucid Screams*, the opening and closing stories were connected. They bookended the collection and a lot of people were fans of how that worked out. I was excited to do it again for *Impulses of a Necrotic Heart*. Picking up a month later after killing his father, Danny goes back to the Cooperstown Estate and his mind quickly deteriorates as he hears his dead father whistling from inside the wall. I've had musical tinnitus twice in my life. It was incredibly strange to hear a song that wasn't playing—and if it had lasted more than a few minutes, it could have easily been maddening. I was stoked to work that idea into a story, and better yet, I get to give a nod to one of my favorite short stories of all time, Edgar Allan Poe's *The Tell-Tale Heart*.

CONTENT WARNINGS

Suicide/Suicidal ideations:

The Haunting of Swan Lake

Here For You

Abduction & Assault (implied)

Sensory Deprivation

Tangerine Sky

Child death, Grieving

Dogwood

Body dysmorphia, Sexual harassment of a child

Don't Make It Weird